Praise for Maria Grace

"Grace has quickly become one of my favorite authors of Austen-inspired fiction. Her love of Austen's characters and the Regency era shine through in all of her novels." ***Diary of an Eccentric***

"Maria Grace is stunning and emotional, and readers will be blown away by the uniqueness of her plot and characterization" ***Savvy Wit and Verse***

"Maria Grace has once again brought to her readers a delightful, entertaining and sweetly romantic story while using Austen's characters as a launching point for the tale." ***Calico Critic***

"I believe that this is what Maria Grace does best, blend old and new together to create a story that has the framework of Austen and her characters, but contains enough new and exciting content to keep me turning the pages. ... Grace's style is not to be missed." ***From the desk of Kimberly Denny-Ryder***

The Attentions of A Most Affectionate Mother

Maria Grace

White Soup Press

Published by: White Soup Press

A Most Affectionate Mother
Copyright © 2018 Maria Grace

For information, address
author.MariaGrace@gmail.com

ISBN-13: 978-0-9997984-0-9 (White Soup Press)

Author's Website: RandomBitsofFaascination.com
Email address: Author.MariaGrace@gmail.com

Dedication

For my husband and sons.
You have always believed in me.

Chapter 1

MAMA TRUNDLED INTO the parlor in another one of her flurries. The sunbeams and dust motes gave way to her, knowing better than to interfere. The furniture would probably scoot out of the way, too, if it could. Kitty jumped up from the faded beige couch, nearly dropping her sewing and looking immensely interested in whatever new intrigue Mama might bring them.

Mary slipped a ribbon into her book and set it aside without sighing. That was an accomplishment all told, considering the reg-ularity of Mama's flurries. There was really no point in trying to read once Mama started to bustle about.

Mama often found reason to flurry and fuss—it was practi-cally a daily occurrence. It felt like her need for commotion had increased since last winter when Jane and Lizzy had married and gone away. With three daughters now out of the house, it appeared she was easily bored, and perhaps her flurries were her way of add-ing some interest to her day. Naturally, it never seemed to occur to her to check if anyone else enjoyed the amusement as much as she.

On the whole, it was generally best to simply pre-tend to pay attention, inserting the appropriate sounds of response here and there as necessary in or-der to convince Mama she was actually be-ing attended, and all the while Mary could go about her own thoughts in the privacy of her mind.

How Jane would scold her for her attitude. But truly, it was the only way to manage Mama these days without biting a hole in one's tongue.

"Kitty, Mary, come around and join me! Come around, come now! The post just arrived, and I have letters from your sis-ters. All of them! Can you imag-ine? Three letters in a single day? I am beside myself with excitement." Mama pulled a chair close to the high oak tea table on the far side of the room and spread out her treasures before her.

That all it took was three letters in a single day to send Mama into convulsions of delight said a great deal. Since that same fact revealed little uplifting or positive, it was probably best not to dwell upon it.

Mary adjusted a simple oak chair near the tea table and sat down, smoothing the tablecloth in front of her. Mary, Kitty and Lydia had embellished the pale yellow linen with violets and dai-sies for Mama as a Twelfth Night gift three years ago. Funny how Mama always seemed to sit at the edge that Lydia had em-broidered with sloppy daisies and lopsided violets.

Bother. That was another ungracious thought. Far too many of them for comfort this morning.

Her sisters' distinct handwriting greeted her from the direc-tions written on the folded letters. Swoopy and exuberant from Lydia. So many curls and loops, mismatched and unruly.

Jane's was dainty and perfectly regular, exactly as all the guidebooks directed that a lady's hand should be. So easy to read, as though not willing to displease anyone by stepping outside the accepted formation of any letter. Yes, that was definitely Jane.

Lizzy's writing was narrow and angular, more di-rect and to the point, if that were possible for handwriting. It was clear and legible, but not as artis-tic and pleasing to look at as Jane's. One read Lizzy's letters because they contained information and were often interesting, not because they were pretty and worthy of fram-ing which, given the occasional lack of content in Jane's letters, was sometimes the best that could be said of them.

Mama cracked the seal on Lydia's missive and un-folded it. Of course, she would start with that one. Mary gritted her teeth as Mama turned her shoulder into a sunbeam to better catch the light on the paper. At least she would get it over with quickly.

"My dear family, I have been ever so busy. Please do not complain that I do not write more often. As a married woman, you must know I am fraught with demands on all sides. I must appor-tion my time most carefully." Mama pressed her palm to her chest, her eyes a little misty. "I am so proud of her, just fifteen and a mar-ried woman! She followed my advice and look what she got."

Mary clenched her jaw. No, a taciturn remark would not do. Those only ignited arguments. Mama did not want to think about all those things that Lydia might be called upon to do be-cause of what she "got." But really, was it not obvious by the fre-quency of Jane's and Lizzy's letters that not all married wom-en were so intolerably busy?

"I am to have a new dress made soon. Wickham has prom-ised me. And I know precisely what I shall have …"

Mary glanced at Kitty who rolled her eyes. Appar-ently she saw it, too. Could Mama not discern Lydia's fantasies from reali-ty?

To be fair, it was probably easier to pick such things out af-ter reading the letters Lizzy had written directly to Mary. It seemed Lydia wrote to her eldest sisters far more frequently than to Mama. In those letters, she often asked for some help for Wickham from Lizzy and Jane's "rich husbands" who doubtless would not miss the blunt much.

It was sad that their youngest sister was in serious straits, barely able to hire a single maid-of-all-work and having to share a house with several other young officers and their wives. Still, it was hardly the condi-tions Lydia described in her communications to her parents. From those, no one would guess she was sharing in the disagreeable household tasks, even con-sidering taking in some sewing or hosting a dame school to teach some children their letters and first reading to bring in a few more coins like the other junior officers' wives were doing.

While it was tempting to simply tell Mama the truth and bring these unpleasant letter-reading ses-sions to an end, it would be too unkind. She would be crushed to learn the reality of Lydia's situation which would probably make things even worse for all of them.

And they would still have to sit through Jane's letters. And yes, it was petty and wrong to find them so displeasing, but she did. If this torment continued on any longer, there was no telling what she would hear herself thinking next!

"Excuse me, Mama." Mary jumped up in the middle of Mama's sentence. "Might we continue this another time? I just re-alized that I must return this book to the library today."

"Oh, Mary. Why did you not take care of the task when you went into town with me yesterday?" There was something a little crestfallen in Mama's tone.

"In the midst of calling upon Aunt Philips, it slipped my mind. Pray forgive me." Mary curtsied, scooped up her book, and scurried for the door.

Kitty half stood, but Mama waved her down. "Let her go." She harrumphed. "But it need not curtail any pleasure of yours, my dear. Let us go on with Jane's letter and hear of her successes, hav-ing followed my directions."

The spring sunshine was bright but not entirely warm yet. The ground had dried enough from the last rain to not be muddy but not so much as to be dusty. A soft breeze blew, not enough to make one blousy, but sufficient to make the light shawl she wore quite necessary. All in all, the perfect sort of weather for a brisk—a very brisk—walk to Clarke's Circulating Library at the far side of Meryton.

It was a small untruth that the book needed to be returned today. While she had finished reading the volume, the errand could have waited. But avoiding a letter from Jane could not.

While it was true, Jane's letters were all sweetness and light, she also went on and on about how excited she was about their time in London and how delightful it would be to move back to the country once matters were settled on the purchase of Bingley's new estate. He was, of course, overjoyed to be fulfilling his father's fondest wish for his family to enter the landed class.

Ugh. What more was there to be said but "ugh?"

Yes, it was wonderful for Jane, and yes, she was truly glad for her sister's good fortune. But did she have to make everything sound like a fairy story? Were there no cross words ever spoken in their home? Did she truly approve of everything that Bingley did?

And did she realize all her letters had the effect of utterly convincing Mama that sending her daughter out in the rain was the right way to get herself a husband? If Mama had been intent upon "helping" her daughters before, now she was just shy of obsessed with it.

At least Lizzy was far more realistic in her descriptions of life at Pemberley. While she did her best to make the foibles of the household laughable, at least it all sounded like a fair representa-tion of real life. Which was probably why Mama rarely took credit for Lizzy's marital success.

No doubt she would be treated to a reprise of all the letters when she returned. But for now, she was free and would enjoy that freedom to the fullest. Not to mention, it would allow her to discharge her promise to Charlotte. That would be no small relief to get off her mind.

As she entered Meryton, she could make out the roofline of Clarke's three-story brick building at the far edge of town. What a refuge that place had become. She had appreciated it when she and Lizzy made their fortnightly visits there. But now, she visited as often as she was able and lingered in the reading room, even occa-sionally partaking of tea there in order to stay a little longer. On some days, she even perused the display case of specialty goods kept to induce young ladies to open their purses to supplement the library's income. Whoever supplied Clarke's had good taste with dainty writing papers, quills, and desk accessories. Why they would carry powder puffs was difficult to discern, but even those were pretty enough to attract Kitty's admiration.

If Meryton had not enjoyed so many visitors and so much traffic from London, they might not have enjoyed a first-rate li-brary. Clarke's boasted not only several storerooms of books, but also a large reading room and a chamber set aside for tea, conver-sation, and games which meant the reading room stayed relatively quiet. What a wonderful place where a respectable woman could be left in peace, alone and undisturbed with her thoughts.

Mary slipped into Clarke's as two chattering young ladies sauntered out, tucking their novels into small baskets and covering them with embroidered napkins. Silly things. If they were ashamed to be reading novels, then why do so in the first place? There was nothing wrong with a good novel now and again. In fact, they were quite diverting and often exactly what one needed to transcend the dreariness of life. But today that was not her mission. What a shame, though. A good novel would have been quite welcome just now.

She drank in a deep breath of book-smell as other patrons milled about. Was not that one of the most soothing fragrances ev-er? Mama and Kitty would disagree—it made them sneeze—probably Jane too, but Lizzy would smile and wink at the thought. Papa's book room smelt like that, too, not that she was allowed in often. He said his collection had little to interest young women and kept the door firmly shut. Even Lizzy had only been allowed to enjoy a few select volumes.

There was something so comforting about a library. Maybe it was that it was one of the rare public spaces a young woman could visit alone without calling her reputation into question. Per-haps it was being surrounded by so much … potential … yes, that was a good word for it. Potential for discovery, for learning, for being transported away from one's mundane life into one much more extraordinary. Whatever it was, it was difficult to conceive of a more delightful place to call upon.

Mary took her place in line at the circulation desk in front of the tantalizing storeroom. No need to peruse the catalog today. "The Moral Miscellany, please."

The clerk's eyebrow rose, but he was well trained enough that he said nothing but scurried to the backroom to find her re-quest.

Yes, Mama and Kitty would tease her over the title, and Papa would raise a brow and tut-tut. Let them think what they would. Charlotte Lucas had recently written to her of Mr. Collins' plan to establish a day school for the boys of Hunsford Parish. He would teach them to read, write, plus a bit of history and the like, and—with Lady Catherine's approbation, or perhaps direct or-ders—he would also ensure the boys' morals were properly estab-lished. Lady Catherine had suggested the use of a particular vol-ume not present in the Hunsford library but available in Meryton. Charlotte had asked Mary to read the tome and take notes that Mr. Collins could then teach from.

In truth, it was an honor to have been asked for assistance and advice, an honor Mary could not take lightly. Yes, perhaps it could be argued that she was taking it all far too seriously. But in such matters, it was better to err on the side of being too concerned and too studious than not enough. After all, the consequences could truly be eternal. Hopefully, the book would be sufficiently interesting to allow her to discharge her burden with appropriate detail and attention. Otherwise, this could be a dreary task indeed.

"Here you are, Miss Bennet." The clerk handed her the dusty volume.

Apparently it was not a popular title. How surprising.

Beside them, another clerk spoke in not-so-hushed tones to an unfamiliar young man. "Pray forgive me, sir, but it seems that young lady has just checked out the very manuscript you have asked for. You will have to wait for her to return it, but I am happy to make a note that you are waiting for it. Is there something else you might be interested in?"

The young man, rather tall and imposing, with a tousled crop of hair that hung down to bushy eyebrows, turned toward her and glowered.

What atrocious manners! Who did he think he was? And, perhaps more disturbing, who did he think she was?

Though certainly inappropriate, Mary met the man's stare with one of her own: cold, dark, and pointed. He blinked and shook his head.

That was satisfying.

She gathered her book to her chest and strode toward the reading room. Best not continue these improper interactions lest he garner the wrong impression of her. She had work to accomplish, and it would not do to allow anything to get in her way.

He followed after her, boots clomping. "Wait, miss, pray stop." Though not raised to a shout, his voice boomed and com-manded. How brazen.

Good manners and good breeding demanded that she stop in the middle of the busy room halfway between the front door and the clerk's desk. So she did, but she did not turn to look at him. "I have not made your acquaintance, sir. Your demand is most impertinent."

He scurried in front of her, his eyes wide and open hands lifted. "Pray wait here a moment." He dashed off toward the read-ing room.

It was a perfect time to make her escape. She really should, though it would be polite to wait just a bit. A minute, nothing more. That crooked longcase clock that stood next to the tea room door and ticked far too loudly would now be her ally rather than merely an irritation. Tick-tock-tick. A moment more and the hand would shift to the next minute, and she would—

"Miss Bennet, how delightful!" Sir William Lucas? What was he doing here? When did he frequent the library?

She nodded at him and forced a pleasing countenance on her face. He was not wearing the Master of Ceremonies sash he so enjoyed donning at local assemblies, but his expression was the one he wore then.

"I have heard you are in want of an introduction." He trun-dled toward her, hands clasped over his ample belly, the unusual young man just behind him. Several young ladies scooted out of their way, staring from the corners of their eyes.

"No, sir. I would not trouble you for such a thing—" She slipped back a step.

"Pray forgive me, sir. I am the one in want of an introduc-tion." The young man bowed slightly. "It is my understanding that this young lady is in your circle of acquaintance."

"Indeed, she and her family are. We consider them great friends." Sir William gestured broadly as though proving his point. His round, red cheeks seemed to punctuate his too-loud smile.

Mary held her breath to avoid a sigh. He might consider them great friends, but she was not so generous. It was still some-thing of a sore point that Mr. Collins had chosen Charlotte over her.

All the more reason why she needed to do this favor for Charlotte. It would prove, at least to herself, that she was past her resentments and ill-feelings.

"Miss Bennet, may I introduce Mr. Percy John-stone, Vicar of Hetherington Parish." Sir William thumbed his lapels and rocked forward on his toes.

Was there any other man who could be so pleased in offering so simple a service?

Mr. Johnstone bowed.

She curtsied because it was appropriate. "I am pleased to make your acquaintance, sir." It was difficult to lie without letting her expression betray her.

What matter, it probably made no difference. Not that Sir William would notice, and if this Mr. Johnstone did, it was good for him to understand how welcome this acquaintance was.

"As am I, madam." He bowed from his shoulders. His pleasant tone seemed as forced as hers.

If he did not want to know her, then why was he so deter-mined to obtain an introduction? How maddening could he con-trive to be?

"Very good, very good. I see my task here is done." Sir William patted his belly and lumbered off, no doubt to find another good deed to do for some unsuspecting innocent.

"Er, ah, Miss Bennet, now that we have been properly ac-quainted … about my book." He glanced about furtively and pointed to the ill-gotten treasure she clutched to her chest.

"Your book, sir?" She clasped it a little tighter and slipped back another step. "You are quite presumptuous. By all rights, this volume belongs to Clarke's, not to you. And I have rightfully checked it out. There is no means by which you can argue that this item is yours."

"What need have you for such a title? It is hardly a wom-an's kind of reading." His nose wrinkled into a sort of a sneer.

If she had any inkling to be sympathetic to him, he had now lost it. "That is not for you to judge. Why else would a woman come to a library but to read what books she pleases? I would thank you to keep your opinions to yourself. I have never asked for them, and I can tell you, without reservation, that I do not welcome them."

His eyes buldged, an expression that in other circumstances might have been funny. The furrowed creases on his forehead deepened, a bit like one of Gillray's caricatures. "I need that book."

"And I do not? Why else would I have taken it out?" Both-er! She was nearly shouting now.

"What do you need it for?"

"That is a personal question and hardly any of your busi-ness."

"My requirement is greater." He took a long stride toward her.

She backpedaled to match. "I am sure that in your eyes, your needs are always greater than anyone else's."

He cocked his head and blinked. Could he really be sur-prised? "That is a harsh judgement."

"Have you given me any reason to think otherwise of you?"

He clutched his forehead, rolling his eyes. He was as dra-matic as Lydia when she did not get her way. "Pray return the book, and let me have it."

"You may have it when I have finished with it. Besides, since I have already checked it out, I have used all my subscription for the month, and I will have to wait a full fortnight before I might take out another."

"That is easily remedied. I will pay for you to extend your subscription this month." He patted a coat pocket that must contain his purse.

"That is a grand gesture, I am sure, but I do not know you at all. I cannot possibly accept a gift even under these circumstanc-es. I will assume that it was well-meant, but I will not endanger my reputation for your convenience. Good day." She turned sharply on her heel and marched out of the library.

Two young women dodged out of her way. She threw the door open and charged into the sunshine.

The audacity of the man! The gall! Pompous, arro-gant crea-ture, demanding she give up her rightfully-obtained tome to him simply because he declared that he needed it more than she. Who was he to make that judgement? Worse still, who was he to make a public offer to pay for her subscription?

She pressed a hand to her belly to subdue the sick feeling. What might people think after hearing that? Her cheeks burned. At least Sir William would vouch for her decency.

What an audacious, ill-mannered sort of man was this vicar from Hetherington.

More offensive, he had cheated her out of her time in the reading room, time she had desperately needed. How could she possibly return home now with all her sensibilities whipped into frenzy? Oh, the things that would slip from her lips! Mama and Kitty might never recover from the shock. No, she needed some-place to collect herself before facing Longbourn again.

She turned away from the library toward the baker's. She had nothing to do there, but the smell of baking breads was always calming, exactly what she required. She paused near the doorway, soaking in the perfume of hot, yeasty pastries, and licked her lips. Perhaps a Chelsea bun....

"Pray, Miss Bennet, please wait." No! He was like a dog begging for scraps.

She whirled toward him. "Pray, importune me no further, sir. I regret Sir William introduced us at all. Pray do not make me resort to cutting you in public."

"I regret that those are your feelings on the matter. But, I beseech you, hear me out. I am in desperate need of that book. I am about to start a school, and one of my patrons … ah … request-ed … that I use that exact title in my teaching. I have little choice but to make some use of it in planning my students' lessons."

"I am on a similar mission for the wife of Hunsford's vicar. They have the same need."

"Oh." His jaw dropped, his mouth forming a round "o." He looked at his feet.

Perhaps now he was convinced that she truly needed the text. Not that she should have had to defend her choice of reading material to a complete stranger. "You will excuse me now." She bent her knees in a tiny curtsey and tried to edge past him.

"That changes nothing for me. How long will you have it?" At least his voice had lost its commanding-demanding edge.

"As long as I need. I think that is longer now than when you first began to harass me over it." The latter bit probably was unnecessary and even unkind, but had she not been driven to it?

"Please, madam …"

"I will not give up my book."

His shoulders slumped. Why did he have to look like a kicked puppy?

She huffed. "But if you are so desperate to use it, you may speak to my father. Perhaps he will consent to you using it in his library when I am not reading it myself. Now, good day."

His lifted his head and stared at her, slack-jawed, as though trying to find words.

She nodded as she strode away, listening for footsteps. Good, there were none.

Hopefully that would keep the blackguard away from her and her book.

Chapter 2

Three days later, Mary sat in the parlor, The Moral Miscel-lany open in a morning sunbeam on the writing desk. Empty as it was now, the parlor felt spacious with seating that would easily accommodate at least eight, not including the writing desk by the window. Pale yellow walls magnified the sunlight while soft breezes floated in, teasing the light curtains into an elegant dance. It really was a pleasant room.

She looked down at the cross-written sheet of paper before her. Her handwriting was not nearly as pretty as Jane's or as legible as Lizzy's, but given the magnitude of the favor Charlotte asked, reading her hand was little to ask. No doubt that was all she would receive in return for her time spent with Mr. T. Cadell and his *Moral Miscellany*.

What an unkind, disagreeable, inappropriate

thought. It was an honor to do such a favor for her friend. No reward was needed or even appropriate—even when a very great deal was being asked of her.

She sanded the page and stood. Gracious heavens, it took far longer to cover those first several essays than she had expected. Certainly this was much more serious reading than the nursery sto-ries about cats and dogs and birds that she remembered. How this work might be used to instruct children still eluded her. On the Omniscience and Omnipresence of the Deity, together with the Immensity of his Works did not seem to be the sort of thing her Gardiner neph-ews would be able to attend to, much less under-stand. But, she had not been asked to evaluate the text, only to summarize it for use.

She stretched her shoulders and her neck. How long had she been at this? Several hours now. It was definitely time for a break. Charlotte would not be expecting her response to be posted for at least a week, so she had the luxury of a little time. Especially considering that the book was not due back to the library until after that.

Was it so wrong to plan on keeping it for the full duration of her rental? Probably. If nothing else, it was a little petty. Not a pretty trait in a woman. She really did need to put more effort into adjusting her attitudes.

A flash of movement at the window caught her eye. She pulled the curtain aside, pressing the side of her face to the win-dowpane. What was that? Was there a caller expected today? Sure-ly that was a man's coat coming up the front walk. But Papa re-ceived few callers.

A loud knock summoned Mrs. Hill to the front

door. Low voices murmured just beyond the parlor door. Mrs. Hill's she could identify, but the other, a man's voice, she could not. Mrs. Hill's footsteps trailed off toward Papa's study and, a moment later, back again.

"He will see you," Hill traipsed back toward Papa's bookroom.

How decidedly odd. Who would be visiting—

Kitty scurried into the parlor and pressed the door shut be-hind her. "Mary! Mary! You will never guess!" She clutched her hand to her chest, breathing hard, every inch a novel's romantic heroine.

Mary looked at the ceiling where the plaster was cracked and looked as though it was held together by cobwebs. "Then why do you not tell me?"

"Why must you be that way? You are always such a kill-joy." Kitty rolled her eyes and flounced to the settee near the fire-place. "I have seen the oddest thing. A strange man has come to call on Papa!"

"I gathered that much, sitting here and hearing the door open."

"But I am sure you did not see him," Kitty taunted in her best singsong.

"Is there a reason I might want to?"

Kitty rose and sashayed to Mary. "I think he was rather handsome, in a tousled, windblown sort of way."

"Since the day is quite calm, that hardly sounds like a com-pliment." Mary turned her back on Kitty, not that it would do much good.

"Why are you determined to dislike everything?" Kitty stomped.

"Why are you so determined to find everything agreeable even before you know its nature?" And why could she not mind her own business?

"His nature, you mean."

"You sound like Lydia."

"What is so bad about that? She was the first among us to get herself a husband." The edge of Kitty's lips curled up in a little sneer.

"And such a husband she got. I would enjoin you not to follow her example." Mary dragged her hand down her face. Kitty's hero-worship of Lydia was worse than she had realized.

"Mama is right! You are jealous. Spiteful and jealous that you will end up an old maid, and she, the youngest of us all—"

Mary clapped her hand over her eyes. So that is what Mama thought of her. "You do realize she is constantly begging Jane and Elizabeth for pennies because her husband drinks away all their money."

"That is a lie! Did you not see her last letter?" Kitty sound-ed like Mama when she shrieked.

"Perhaps I should let you read her letters to me. Only last month she asked if I had any pocket money—"

Kitty leaned into Mary's face. "I do not believe you. I will not hear this. In fact, I will tell Mama the lies you are spreading about Lydia!"

"Pray do not tell her!"

"See there, that is proof you are lying."

"No, I am trying to protect Mama. It would devastate her to know Lydia is not enjoying the kind of life to which she had grown accustomed."

"Liar!"

Mary pinched the bridge of her nose and sighed. There was no reasoning with Kitty in this state. Mary shook her head and qui-etly removed herself from the parlor.

The closed door muffled Kitty's protests but did not silence them. For that, one would probably need to leave the house.

A walk in the rose garden would not be a bad thing, and if she took a large basket and shears, she could make an excuse to Mama that she intended to cut flowers for the vases while she was out. Granted, that might not be her first purpose, but it would be worth doing for the relief of getting out. Yes, that was a very good idea.

Papa intercepted her near the kitchen on the way to the still room. "Ah, excellent, I was looking for you. Pray join me in the study." He nodded and turned back toward his bookroom.

It would have been pleasing for him to deign to wait for her response, but few were offered that sort of privilege. Swallowing back another sigh, she followed him through the dimly-lit corridor to his crowded study.

"Mary, this is Mr. Percy Johnstone, Vicar of Hetherington Parish." Papa gestured toward his guest, sitting in one of the two large leather wingchairs near the fireplace.

He looked as he had at the library: slightly more than windblown but slightly less than untidy, just on the edge of un-kempt. The effect was no more attractive here than when they had first met.

"I have made his acquaintance." She crossed her arms over her chest and planted her feet firmly.

"Yes, I understand, Sir William introduced you at Clarke's." Why was Papa smiling so wryly?

"Good morning, Miss Bennet." Mr. Johnstone stood and bowed from his shoulders. At least his manners were improving.

"Good day, sir." No matter how she felt, it would not do to be rude. "What brings you to see my father today?"

"Well, now, after a fashion, you did offer an invitation." Mr. Johnstone's left eye twitched, and the corner of his lips lifted to match.

Impertinent! She stomped toward him. "Excuse me, but I did not. I have only met you once. I would not offer so bold an invitation."

Papa cleared his throat, but it sounded alarmingly like there was a laugh underneath it. "Forgive me, Mary, but I must argue. I believe you did just that."

Mary gasped. "What do you mean?"

"Unless Mr. Johnstone is quite a fanciful liar which I will admit is still a real possibility—" Papa's eyebrow flashed up a mite.

Mr. Johnstone snickered.

"I am under the impression you said something to the effect of, 'If you are so desperate for the use of the book I have checked out, speak to my father. Perhaps he will consent to you using it in his library when I am not reading it myself.' That sounds very much like an invitation to me." Papa glanced at Mr. Johnstone in a way that might be regarded conspiratorial.

Mary's face flushed all the way down to her shoulders. Horrible man, taking her literally in a moment of unchecked frus-tration. Any reasonable person would not have taken that as an in-vite—would they?

"And he has done so." Now Papa smiled openly.

She looked away. "Apparently."

"I would not have had the audacity to make such a petition had you not suggested it yourself." The way

Mr. Johnstone's eyes twinkled—he was laughing at her!

"I am sure you would not have." No, he would probably ra-ther have ripped the book from her hands and run off with it.

"I have heard his application for access to the volume in question. His reasons are quite as sound as yours. Moreover, he must return to his own parish soon and does not have the luxury of waiting for you to be finished." The sharp edge to Papa's voice implied disapproval. "So I have agreed to your proposal."

Her heart thudded in her throat so hard she could barely speak.

"He may use the book here in my study when you are not engaged with it. I believe the concept is called 'sharing.'"

"But, how can you—"

"I doubt you will feel any inconvenience at all. I have noted that you are apt to read early in the day before you mother pays her morning calls. Then you either go with her, or you go off to pay your own or venture to town or take advantage of the afternoon sun to work on your sewing. You are a creature of habit, you know."

She pressed her hands to her cheeks. How could he know her schedule so well? When had he ever paid so much attention to what she did?

"If he comes at a time similar to today, I expect you will have finished your daily reading and will hardly be inconvenienced by sharing the book with Mr. Johnstone."

She wrapped her arms around her waist. "It appears that what I think hardly matters."

Papa cleared his throat again, but this time there was no laugh underlying it.

He was right. She was bordering on rude, but he—both of them—were little better.

"The book is in the parlor if you want it. I am going out to cut flowers for Mama." She tossed her head and stormed out of the study.

For the next four days, Mr. Johnstone appeared like clock-work at half past eleven every morning, exactly the time she was most likely to quit her studies and turn to other pursuits. Some days, just to be contrary, she lingered another quarter of an hour, but it never proved profitable. She stared at words and scratched her pen along the paper, but no real insights were gained through the effort.

Through it all, Mr. Johnstone never complained nor even looked cross at being made to wait. He had even taken up a game of chess with Papa whilst he waited. Surely it was an intentional ploy to be that much more irritating. What else could it be?

When she finished her studies, she would knock on Papa's door and hand him the volume, saying little to him and nothing to Mr. Johnstone whenever possible which thankfully was usually the case.

Saturday morning, though, she found herself particularly vexed by Mr. Johnstone's presence and decided to pay a call on Maria Lucas to soothe her raw nerves.

Granted, on most days this sort of venture would hardly have been a balm. Maria was more Kitty and Lydia's friend than she was Mary's, and her attitudes and opinions matched theirs. But today, any company away from Longbourn was welcome.

Since Lady Lucas was already entertaining a guest, Maria suggested a walk through Lady Lucas' gardens was in order. For all her other foibles, Lady Lucas was a remarkable gardener, able to coax the shyest sort of flowers from the soil and into the sun. The flower beds were arranged along a winding path, ebbing and flowing in the spring sunshine.

"Who has called upon your mother? I do not recognize her." Mary drew a deep breath filled with the heavy perfume of many blossoms. Bees buzzed among the stalks, their hum hanging in the air.

Maria stooped to smell a tall coneflower. "She is our vicar's sister, Mrs. Johnstone. She is visiting with her son from Heth-erington Parish. I am surprised you have not met her."

"No, I have not had the pleasure." Mary scuffed her toes in the gravel.

"Kitty said that Mr. Johnstone has been calling upon your father nearly every day, I should have thought—" There it was, that wheedling tone, trying to pry information without actually asking anything.

"Well, your thought was wrong."

"Gracious, you need not snap at me so. It is not as if I have said anything untoward. What is making you so touchy? Kitty says you have been mightily unpleasant recently. Have you not been introduced to Mr. Johnstone? I hear he is quite handsome." Maria leaned over to look into Mary's face.

Mary turned away. "I do not find him so."

"Really? Then you have met him."

"He has been to see my father. Of course, I have met him. And I am singularly unimpressed." Mary pressed forward along the path.

Tall stalks arched across the pathway as though

reaching to brush shoulders with her. Some of them showered her with petals as she walked past. How welcome they made her feel.

Unlike Maria.

"Then you seem to be the only one in town of that opinion. All the girls are wild to be introduced to him." Maria clasped her hands and batted her eyes as though longing for such an introduc-tion.

"I do not see why."

"Then you surely cannot see past the end of your nose. Yesterday he brought some of his young cous-ins into town for a trip to the confectioner. You should have seen him with the chil-dren. I cannot im-agine a dearer sight to behold. He was so kind and gentle with them. Even you would have been im-pressed."

Mary paused mid-step. "Indeed? I would never have ex-pected...."

"Nor, I imagine, would you have anticipated the kindness and deference he shows to his poor mother who is half-deaf and blind and walks with a cane. He is the picture of patience and grace with her." Why did Maria have to wear that smug expression?

"It seems as though we are talking about two en-tirely dif-ferent men." Was it possible there were two newcomers to Meryton with similar names?

"It does, does it not? How have you found him to be?" There was that gossipy plea again.

"Quite different from what you describe."

"How? Tell me?" Maria stepped directly in front of Mary and blocked her steps.

"No. No, I fear that would become gossip very quickly, and I do not want to venture into that."

"There you go again, moralizing to everyone. How

interest-ing when it seems that perhaps you have judged someone unfairly, you will not even consider the possibility." Maria crossed her arms over her chest, a triumphant glimmer in her eyes.

"Pray excuse me. I should go." Mary curtsied and hurried away from Maria and Lucas Lodge.

Maria may have called after her, but it was hard to tell with the storm of thoughts in her mind and the tall stems determined to block her way. They taunted and teased her until she broke out into an unladylike run.

Was it possible all that Maria said was true? Why would she make it up, though? Maria was the last person to go out of her way to find positive things to say about a newcomer. Was that not why Mary sought her out today, to find someone who might share her low opinion of Mr. Johnstone even if Maria had not met him herself?

She broke out of the garden into an open field. The field grasses whispered along her skirts, little burrs catching at her hem and tugging her back. Mary's eyes burned, and her vision blurred. How humiliating—being shown so in error by Maria Lucas.

Mary had always prided herself on her propriety and pen-chant for proper thought and behavior next to Maria, Kitty and the other girls of their cohort. Now to be shown wanting next to her? The shame of it! It was almost too much.

Mary sat down on the stile step. Not almost too much, it was too much. She covered her face with her hands and wept. Eve-rything she looked down upon and disliked the most, she had be-come. Judgmental, gossip-mongering, self-righteous. Those vices which she had not thought possible in herself, they were there in full force. And Maria Lucas and Mr. Johnstone made them clear to her. The shame!

The sun was past its zenith when her tears finally dried. While cathartic, tears would hardly resolve anything. No, that would require more effort on her part. If she found fault with her own character, there was only one way that would change. She must confront it and intentionally choose a different, a better, path.

It would take work, a determined effort. But she could do it. If she had any hope of being able to live with herself, she had to.

At least she had not been directly rude to him and had no public behavior to apologize for. That made it a wee bit easier to face.

Just a bit.

But nothing more was to be resolved here out in the fields. She dried her cheeks with her apron and stood, brushing the cling-ing grass blades away.

"Miss Bennet!"

She looked up and jumped back. "Mr. Johnstone!" She grabbed the stile and clung to it for support.

He seemed genuinely flustered. "Pray forgive me. I had no idea you were there. I should have looked more carefully where I was going."

Yes, he should have, but that was a curt and judgmental thought. "There is no harm done. You had no reason to expect someone to be on the other side of the stile."

He backed up a little and brushed his jacket. "Still, I should have been more attentive. Pray excuse me. I was rushing to return to my mother who is visiting at Lucas Lodge this afternoon."

"So I understand. I was there not long ago myself, calling upon their daughter, Maria." She looked over her shoulder toward Lucas Lodge.

"I was introduced to her this morning. She seems like a pleasant girl." That was the right thing to say, but was it really what he thought?

"She is a good friend of my younger sisters."

He nodded and stared past her, vaguely uncomfortable.

Mary looked behind her. "Is someone approaching? I see no one there."

"No, no, I am sorry. It is a bad habit of mine." He worried his hands together. "I suppose there is no better way here than to be direct."

"Excuse me?" Now it was her turn to stare.

"Your mother has invited me to Longbourn for dinner to-night. I have not yet made a reply, though."

Oh, of course she did! How could Mama possibly let es-cape the opportunity to meddle? "I fear I do not follow you."

"It seems we, you and I, have been on difficult terms since we met at the library." He turned his eyes down toward his boots.

Mary swallowed hard and nodded.

"I can only guess that my presence at the dinner table would be unpleasant to you. I would not want to make your even-ing uncomfortable. I have already been trespassing upon your hos-pitality every day to make my studies. To impose upon you more seems the height of ingratitude." How sincere he looked, staring mostly at his feet, but occasionally glancing up to her face.

Perhaps Maria had a point. He was not wholly disagreeable to look at.

No better time than now to make good upon her resolve. She straightened her spine and drew a deep breath. "Pray forgive me, for I have been rather of a short temper recently. All the study on behalf of Hunsford's vicar has left me rather out of sorts." There, she admitted it. Let him hate her for it if he dared, but the truth was out now.

His lips twisted into a wry little half-smile. "Since your work will be used in the education of children, I can well under-stand the weight of the burden you carry. Not to mention some of those essays are, shall we say, not the most inspiring things we have ever read?"

She pulled back a mite and looked directly into his eyes, but they did not contradict the soft and concilia-tory tone of his words. Was this the same man who had been vexing her all these days?

"Perhaps it is a burden we might share? If you would in-dulge me in a bit of conversation after din-ner tonight?"

"I … I would be pleased to bring word to my mother that you will join us tonight."

"Only if you would be pleased by my company." His eyes were quite insistent.

"I … I would enjoy talking to you about our shared bur-den," she stammered like a schoolgirl.

He stared at her a moment longer and shrugged as though deciding to be satisfied with her answer. "This evening, then." He smiled and bowed, then proceed-ed on his way toward Lucas Lodge.

Though he might think her answer odd, it was ac-tually quite sincere. It would be a pleasure to talk to someone who truly understood what was on her mind and presumably cared about it as much as she. More-over, it would be unique, perhaps the first time it had ever happened. And that could prove very interesting indeed.

She hummed to herself as she hurried home to tell Mama to expect a guest for dinner..

Chapter 3

"I MUST SAY that is very odd, very odd indeed." Mama pranced around the parlor in a little circle between the tea table and settee, wings flapping, feathers fluffing. The sun cast long shadows across the faded carpet. She was about to work herself into another flurry. "Why could he not have simply accepted the invitation when I offered it?"

"I do not know, Mama." It was a bold-faced lie, but she could hardly tell Mama the truth, could she? That would lead to nothing good for any of them. She smoothed her skirt over her lap and looked out the window from her place on the couch. "I sup-pose he wanted to be certain that his mother would be well-cared for whilst he was away."

"I suppose. I suppose. It is a caring and noble gesture to be sure. One that should be pleasing no doubt.

But it is rather incon-venient." Mama wrung her hands.

Mary turned her face aside a little further so Mama would not see her long-suffering expression. "How so? I can scarcely im-agine your preparations for din-ner will be so different with just one addition to the party."

"But he is not family." Mama whirled toward her and glared. "It is the first time he will have dined with us. One must make a favorable impression when one invites a guest for the first time. Have I taught you nothing?"

"He has been at the house nearly every day this week. It is not exactly the first time he has sat with us." Besides, he was com-ing for conversation, not food, though Mama would never believe that.

"It will be the first time he dines with us. A dinner invita-tion is no small thing, my dear. The impression we make could be a vital one." There was Mama's pointing finger waggling at her as though she had not heard this sort of speech at least a dozen times be-fore.

Mary rolled her eyes toward the ceiling. "Oh, pray, Mama, you have not already decided to make a match with him?"

"He is a respectable young gentleman with quite a good liv-ing. I think either of you girls would do for him quite well." Ma-ma's open hands bounced at her waist, settling the matter.

"Excuse me?" Kitty? With the young vicar? Mary stood.

"What is so astonishing about that? You both are pretty enough when you make the effort. Your man-ners are pleasing, and you are gently-born. As to accomplishments, you are both well-versed in how to manage a household. What more could a clergy-man like him want?"

Mary threw her hands in the air and paced in front of the window. "What more might one want? An agreeable companion? A friend? One of like mind and interests? More practically, one who finds his home and parish acceptable? Did you know he means to run a school out of his home? Can you imagine Kitty in such a situation?"

"All those things can be accomplished if one sets her mind on it." There was Mama's finger again. "The key is having the op-portunity to do so. Just because I managed to see your sisters well-married does not mean you can sit back and ignore all I am doing for you. You cannot assume they will be happy to care for a spin-ster sister."

Mama's faith in her was heartwarming.

"Do not look at me that way, girl. You know how many young ladies never find a husband. Charlotte Lucas nearly joined that number. She was fortunate to have settled well. Do not expect that you can simply sit back and enjoy her good luck. That is not the way of the world. You must try and put yourself out as she did. Seize a chance when it presents itself."

So that is what Mama saw? An opportunity and Mary as something in need of being fixed? "I do not need you pushing Mr. Johnstone or any man at me. Thank you very much." Mary folded her arms and turned her back.

"Well, there is still Kitty. I am sure she will be more sensi-ble than you and make an effort at being pleasing."

Mary turned back to face her. "Kitty is entirely un-suitable for a man like him. She is a … a silly little flirt who cannot hold a serious thought in her head. He is a deep reader, a thinking man, not in want of a frivo-lous companion."

Mama's eyebrows flashed up, and the corners of her lips lifted a mite. "Go get yourself dressed for dinner. Your newest frock will do nicely, I think."

"I have no intention of dressing for dinner. That would suggest—"

"Nothing but common courtesy. Look at you, covered in burrs and mud from your walk. It would be disgraceful, not only our guest, but to all of us, for you to appear at the table like that." Mama gestured at her hem.

Sadly, she was right. "Very well. But not my new-est dress."

Mama snorted. "Very well, your second best will do."

Mary turned on her heel and stormed out.

Mama's desperation to marry her and Kitty off should have subsided with the security that Jane and Elizabeth's excellent matches provided. If anything, considering Lydia's situation, Ma-ma should want to be assured of the character and situation of any young man she might push them towards. But no, it did not seem to occur to her. Marriage at nearly any cost seemed her only goal.

Mary slowly climbed the stairs. She had promised herself to make better efforts toward thinking well of others, and it was time to hold herself to that prom-ise.

Was Mama really so mercenary? It was possible Mama re-alized that Mr. Johnstone was the nephew of their vicar. That mu-tual acquaintance could offer some recommendations as to his na-ture. So, perhaps, she did have more than a passing knowledge of his character. There was something comforting in that thought.

Even so, this was not going to turn into one of Mama's matchmaking affairs.

Absolutely not.

He was an agreeable young man with whom she shared a mutual interest. Nothing more. Absolutely nothing.

An hour and a half later, Mary—in her second best gown, a pretty, blue-sprigged muslin—returned to the parlor to await the arrival of their guest.

About a quarter of an hour later, Kitty flitted into the parlor in her best gown, at Mama's insistence no doubt, cheeks flushed pink—she probably had been pinching them. How silly she looked, so pleased with herself and assured of being pleasing. Ridiculous little flirt.

Papa sauntered in, a contented look on his face. Did he per-haps expect "sensible" conversation at the dinner table tonight? Since Lizzy's departure, he often complained at the lack of it. Not that he tried very hard to engage anyone in it. If he had been will-ing to listen to her, even just a little, he might have been surprised at what he would find.

But that did not signify now. Nor was it in keeping with her promise.

A sharp knock on the door, and Hill ushered Mr. Johnstone into the parlor. He looked much as he al-ways did: a bit tousled and frowsy, but his coat had been brushed and his boots cleaned, so he was taking some trouble to be presentable.

"We are delighted you could join us for dinner, sir." Mama rose and curtsied.

Mary winced at her honeyed tone. Did anyone else hear it that way, or was it her cynicism?

"I thank you for your kind invitation." Mr. Johnstone bowed and sat on the couch that Mama gestured toward between Kitty and Mary.

How utterly unexpected.

"I understand your mother was visiting with Lady Lucas today." Mama settled herself back into her favorite floral uphol-stered chair between the settee and couch.

"Yes. It seems that they share a common acquaintance in town and were encouraged by her to become acquainted." He glanced from Mary to Kitty to Mama, not quite sure where to look.

"How nice. I am sure Lady Lucas is glad for the company. How does your mother find our little slice of Hertfordshire?" Ma-ma's face tightened as it often did when the subject of the Lucases came up.

"I think she has been enjoying it a great deal. She favors a quiet sort of country life, but she declares it is pleasant to be near a village larger than Hetherington. It seems that the shops at Meryton offer a great many wares she cannot easily come by in our little parish."

"There is a great deal to be said for a quiet country exist-ence." Papa leaned back and pressed his elbows into the padded arms of his wingchair. "But one does feel the limits, at times, like the lack of a proper library?" He cocked his head and lifted his eyebrow.

"Indeed, that is a bit of civilization that we sorely miss." Mr. Johnstone chanced a quick glance at Mary.

"I could not agree more." Mama folded her hands in her lap. "It is such an agreeable place for young people to be able to enjoy company. I think the officers of the militia spent many an hour there when they were stationed with us."

Mary covered her eyes with her hand and squeezed her temples. No, she would not comment to that remark. There was no good in it. No, none at all.

"Indeed they did!" Kitty brought her hands together just short of a clap. "They were so handsome in their uniforms. They made Clarke's ever so much more interesting. I am sure you agree, Mary."

Hill arrived with the news that dinner was ready. Was it wrong to be relieved that particular line of discussion was at an end? Mama ushered them to the dining room.

For all her other foibles, Mama did set an excellent table and dining room to match. Flowers, mirrors, and crystal all com-bined to create an atmosphere of comfortable warmth and ease. She could make the room formal when the occasion demanded it, but today, it was cozy and encouraging of conversation.

Mama announced the dishes, and Hill brought around plates of soup. Cauliflower. Made from the leftovers of the vegeta-ble from dinner last night. It was good household management and made for a tasty dish but was not the sort of thing one mentioned in front of guests.

"So what did you think of Clarke's Library?" Kitty asked, smoothing her napkin over her lap.

Mary winced. Apparently that topic was not concluded.

To his credit, Mr. Johnstone did not even blink. "I think it is a well-stocked establishment and a pleasant one. I can see why many enjoy spending time there."

"When the militia was in Meryton, we went there regularly to see the officers and play cards with them. We all found it most agreeable." Kitty seemed so pleased with herself.

Mr. Johnstone paused as though at a loss for words.

Kitty could have that effect on sensible people.

"Of course, you did, why should you not? Their presence added so much to the appeal of the place. It is a well-known fact that a library cannot survive on books alone. It must have some other form of attraction to bring patrons in to spend their coin. How sad it is that the militia had to move on to Brighton to contin-ue with their training and things. We all miss their company sorely. My youngest daughter, you know, married one of their officers."

The creases beside Mr. Johnston's eyes tightened. "I had heard something of that nature."

No doubt he had heard a great deal from Lady Lu-cas on the matter. She was known to bring it up whenever she could. Charlotte's successes were all the brighter when compared to a story like Lydia's.

"It is a lovely thing to have three daughters married, all in one year, you know. We are blessed." Mama flashed a smile at Pa-pa who kept his expression quite neutral.

"So it would appear, madam. My younger sister is unmar-ried and is a constant source of concern to my mother." Mr. John-stone sipped his wine, perhaps basking in his cleverness in changing the topic.

"Does your sister live with you?"

"No, my mother is gracious enough to keep house for me. My sister divides her time between my elder brothers' homes. The eldest holds the estate in Sussex. My second brother is a barrister in London."

Mama clasped her hands before her. "Oh, a barrister! That seems like rather a smart career, especially as it keeps him in town."

"He finds it quite agreeable. It appears to suit his tempera-ment well." Mr. Johnstone pushed a piece of mutton around his plate. What was it about his brother that made him do that?

"And you find the clergy suits yours?" Papa dabbed a drop of soup from his chin with his napkin.

The question seemed to cheer him. "I do, sir. I have been accused more than once of being a bookish sort. It seems a procliv-ity to study is socially acceptable when one is a clergyman."

"Oh, that does sound disagreeable, to be constantly stuck in a room with books." Kitty sniffed.

To her credit, Mama glowered at Kitty. Mr. Johnstone sneaked a long-suffering look toward Mary. Good, he was not of-fended; instead, he seemed amused. Kitty's attitudes were really not worth taking offense at.

"I enjoy scholarship, Miss Kitty. I am looking forward to moving ahead with a plan to start taking in some boys to teach."

"You wish to start a school?" Kitty shuddered. "To have strange children running about underfoot and no governess to mind them? I think it sounds rather dreadful." Her expression suggested she felt it was a great deal more than "rather dreadful."

"But the privilege of shaping young minds that will then in turn have the chance to profoundly impact those around them. What greater influence could a common person have in the world?" The words tumbled out before Mary could stop them.

"I quite agree with you, Miss Bennet."

They locked gazes, but the intensity of the connection was too much to maintain for more than a few seconds.

"I understand there is a particular library book in Mr. Ben-net's possession that you are using in your endeavors?" Mama's eyebrows lifted a little conspiratorially.

"Mary has that one rented out from the library, not I." Papa shrugged over a large bite of potatoes.

"I know she has made it most inconvenient to you, insist-ing she has first use of the tome every morning." Mama snorted. "I do not see why you cannot use it together. I am sure she would benefit from your insight and wisdom as she studies. With all your learning, I am certain you could be of great assistance to her."

And there it was. Leave it to Mama; she could always find a way to meddle. No matter what, that was assured. Mary ground her teeth until they ached. There was absolutely nothing she could say right now that would be profitable. Nothing.

Mr. Johnstone's blush appeared quite sincere. That was some comfort. "I thank you for the compliment, madam. I could not impose upon your daughter's good graces so much. It is enough that she has agreed to share the book with me."

"Nonsense. I understand you are to leave in what, a week? You must be permitted as much time as you like with the material when you have so important a task before you." Mama folded her hands on the table near her plate. The issue, at least in her mind, was settled. The only remaining question was how long it would take everyone else to agree.

"No, madam. Pray, do not trouble yourself." He lifted open hands above the table.

"I insist. We will expect you here as early as you care to come. Mary will—" What an emphasis she placed on that word! "—be happy to share the book with you and to hear your wisdom on the subjects of which she writes to Charlotte."

Mary's cheeks burned. How lovely it was to be talked about as though one were not in the room.

Mr. Johnston turned to her. "I would not insist on impos-ing. How do you feel about this notion?"

It was a nice gesture—very nice—on his part to be sure, but did he know that after Mama's declaration, they had little choice? Since he did not really know Mama, there was no way that he would know. She gritted her teeth and willed a pleasant expression on her face. "I am sure it will be fine. At least, we can make the attempt."

He smiled tentatively, glancing from Mary to Mama. "Then I shall accept your invitation, and as Miss Bennet suggests, we shall try and see how it works."

"Excellent, excellent." Mama settled into her seat like a hen on her nest and tucked into the generous slice of meat on her plate, so very satisfied.

Mary held her breath lest she sigh. On the positive side, though, now they would have plenty of time for conversation. That might not be entirely bad.

As usual, Mary arose shortly after sunrise. The rose-colored beams streaming through her window would normally have elicited at least half an hour spent contemplating the sunrise. A surprising number of good ideas seemed available to one at sunrise. But no such luxury could be enjoyed today.

No, today she looked forward—she grumbled under her breath—to entertaining a guest at an utterly uncouth hour, all at her mother's behest. To his credit, Mr. Johnstone had done his best to excuse himself from the invitation—though upon reflection, Mama's invitation was hardly polite enough to be called an invitation. It was a demand, pure and simple. And no one really ever got away from one of Mama's demands.

It would not be fair of her to hold it against him. Really, it would not. Yet, that was precisely what she most wanted to do. If he had not presented himself daily the prior week to study from her library book, Mama would never have gotten the idea. So in actuality, it was his fault.

But, on the other hand, he could not have possibly known what it was like to give Mama an idea. No one who actually knew such things ever dared. The consequences were too dear. Mary re-ally ought to give him the benefit of the doubt.

She sighed and stared at her closet. Her favorite morning dress called to her. Soft and comfortable, without fuss or nearly any decoration, it was an easy and undemanding gown. That was what she wanted to wear. But no, if she appeared out of her room in that when a gentleman was to arrive, Mama would become posi-tively unhinged. Though not nearly so comfortable, her walking dress would satisfy Mama and avoid the sort of scene Mary dread-ed, so she reached for that.

No sooner had she dressed and made her way down the stairs when a firm rap on the front door set her heart fluttering. She dashed into the parlor and sat at the tea table. He was a man of his word, but did he really have to be so punctual about it? Of course he did, for how else could he make himself vexing while appearing so proper?

She smoothed her skirt over her knees. No, it was not a kind thought or even a fair one. Normally, she would not even have considered something so un-charitable. How out of sorts she was. She pressed her eyes with thumb and forefinger. Regardless of how improper it was to entertain company at this hour, it would behoove her to behave with civility. She adjusted her chair so the sunbeam would comfortably reach her book.

Mrs. Hill opened the parlor door. "Mr. Johnstone, as ex-pected, Miss."

Mary snickered under her breath. Hill was not happy about the irregular visitor either. Somehow that was satisfying.

Mr. Johnstone bowed, morning dew still clinging to the la-pels of his coat, and walked toward her. "Good morning, Miss Bennet. Pray forgive the earli-ness of my call. I thought perhaps your mother—"

Mama burst into the room, beaming and effusive as she never was in the mornings. "Mr. Johnstone! How pleased we are to have you this morning. You are very welcome."

He bowed toward Mama, though something about the creases beside his eyes suggested that another, perhaps less gra-cious thought dwelt behind his pleas-ing countenance. "Your invita-tion has been most thoughtful, madam."

"We are immensely fond of guests here at Longbourn. Mary, especially, is so adept at hospitality." Mama shot her a stern look.

Mary tried not to chuckle. If Mr. Johnstone caught that ex-pression, too—how appalled Mama would be, knowing her looks contradicted her words.

"May I have some tea, or perhaps some coffee, or both, sent up to you?"

"Do you have a preference, Miss Bennet?" he asked, turn-ing his shoulder to Mama.

That small attention seemed to please Mama.

"In truth, I prefer chocolate in the morning." It was true, but rather contrary to say so.

"If that is not too much to ask, I do like a good cup of chocolate in the morning, too." He braced his hands on the back of the chair next to her.

Mama paused and blinked, mouth hanging ajar. That should not be nearly so satisfying as it was. "Why yes, certainly, did I fail to mention that? Bless my soul, I must have left that off entirely. Do forgive me. I cannot imagine what I was thinking. I am sure Cook has already started some chocolate." Mama bustled out the door.

Mary cocked her head at him and raised an eyebrow. "You really are fond of chocolate?"

"In truth I am." He almost winked and pulled the chair nearer the table. "So, may I ask, at which chapter are you in your study of A Moral Miscellany?"

"The Natural History of Ants, sir. And you?"

"It does not matter. I shall pick up where you are and return to the chapters I have missed at a later time." He sat down beside her. "A Natural History of Ants, you say? I confess, I did not even notice that chapter." He tapped the title on the page open before them.

"You are not a fan of Natural History, sir?"

"I am not a fan of ants, if I am to be entirely can-did." His neck twitched. "Do you have a great fondness for them?"

It would be rather satisfying to say yes and watch the ex-pression on his face. But even she could not manage to be quite that contrary, at least not this early in the day. "I cannot say that I do. But it seems our esteemed author has rather a fondness for them and for inflicting experiments upon them as well."

"I imagine he also wishes to make them an allego-ry for mankind as well?" His lips wrinkled in something less than ap-proval.

"It has been done before. Did not Aesop do so in his fa-bles?"

"One might argue that Aesop is far livelier reading than that." He looked down at the book.

She must not snicker, although it did not seem that he would mind. "You do not find the text engaging?"

He caught her gaze and held it, hard. "Do you?"

"There are portions of it that I find entirely engag-ing."

"I suppose, then, I asked the wrong question." He propped his elbow on the table and looked directly at her. "Do you expect it will be useful for the purpose for which you are reading it?"

She sighed, not that she meant to, but it was rather impos-sible to subdue it. "That I find rather more questionable."

"Indeed. I am not completely certain all that is within these covers would be entirely … ah …."

"Interesting? Understandable? Instructive?" She offered each option with a raised eyebrow. The words rolled off her tongue easily. She had been considering that same thought for quite some time. But Charlotte had been absolutely specific that no other book be considered for the purpose.

"Yes, in all those cases. At my students' age, I was rather more interested in fairy stories and myths than some of what is de-scribed here." He thumbed the pages, letting them fall slowly un-der his fingers. "Some of these chapters are really quite beyond the understanding of the young, I think."

The pages fell open to the next chapter: Learning: A Proper Ingredient in the Education of a Woman of Quality of Fortune.

Her eyes widened, and she stared at him. What was he about?

"Have you read this chapter?" His voice sounded so inno-cent—too innocent.

"Indeed I have. Many times to be honest." She ducked her head, her face burning like a child caught in mischief.

"And what was your opinion?"

She pressed her lips. A politic answer would be difficult to achieve. "I would agree that it is not the sort of material one ought to be presenting to young children. It is beyond their understand-ing, I think."

"On that I would agree." He lifted the book. "The text does espouse some rather surprising notions." He cleared his throat and read, "'There is another rea-son why those especially who are women of quality, should apply themselves to letters, namely, be-cause their husbands are generally strangers to them. It is a great pity there should be no knowledge in a family.'

It seems he be-lieves that a woman should have learning in case her husband does not."

What was he implying? Mary pressed the back of her hand to her lips and mumbled, "It is indeed an unusual sentiment, sir."

"One I have heard very little of. And listen to this: 'If we look into the histories of famous women, we find many eminent philosophers of this sex.... Learning and knowledge are perfections in us, not as we are men, but, as we are reasonable creatures, in which order of beings the female world is upon the same level with the male.' What an incredibly bold statement he makes here."

She swallowed hard. "Indeed sir, he does."

"Have you written to your friend of it yet?"

She looked away. Surely there was something worth look-ing at through the window—as long as she kept her eyes away from his it would be well. "No, I have not."

"Why might that be?"

She rose and stalked away, her limbs unable to remain still another moment. "I do not believe her husband and master would find the concepts at all appealing. I rather think he would disagree quite strongly." She turned her back on him, facing the far corner.

There were few who would openly and readily agree it seemed. Even Papa, who enjoyed Elizabeth's reading and occa-sionally approved of Mary's bookishness, often muttered about the silliness of the female sex in general and how not one in a hundred could keep a sensible thought in her head.

Heavy footsteps approached as a long shadow covered her. He stood close behind her, too close, far too close. "And you? What is your opinion?"

"I hardly think my opinion matters."

"I think it does." The words hung thick in the air, like mist over the morning fields.

The audacity! To bait her like that, only for the opportunity to lecture why she was wrong. She whirled at him. "If you really must know, I find his position and proposal refreshing and sensi-ble. To be considered rational and reasonable and as capable as a man is an exceptional notion, rarely heard in polite company. I think society at large would be better for it, and it is high time more of our learned folk would take time to consider the reasona-bility of the propo-sition. There, now you have heard me, so censor me as you will. I am not afraid of your rebuke." Her heart slammed against her ribs, shaking her hands and leav-ing her short of breath.

He looked down at her, his expression neither condescend-ing nor condemning. What was he about?

"I am grateful you have shared your position with me, Miss Bennet. I am quite honored that you would put yourself out to ex-press yourself so clearly on a matter which is obviously close to your heart."

She fought to keep her eyes from bulging and her jaw from gaping. Breathe, she must remember to breathe.

"I think your opinion very worthwhile, and, to be honest, I am apt to agree both with you and the au-thor of that particular es-say. I approve of anyone, including women, improving their minds with exten-sive reading in all areas, even the ones not thought suit-able to a woman's education."

Her eyes narrowed. "You mock me."

"I understand why you would say that, but I am discour-aged that you might believe that of me. No, I do not mock you at all. I am entirely genuine. Why would a man prefer to have a fool-ish, illiterate woman by his side when an intellectual equal might be found?"

Some of her tension slipped away, leaving her a little weak. "I have often wondered that. But it seems a common sentiment."

"Come," he gestured toward the chairs near the fireplace, "please, and tell me of what else you have wondered. Perhaps we have been pondering the same questions."

Such an invitation could be a trap, an invitation to criticism and censure. But the gentleness of his voice held the promise of a rare exchange of equal ideas. Normally, she would run from the risk, but this morning, it seemed worthwhile to take the chance.

Chapter 4

THE NEXT SEVERAL days provided conversation the likes of which she had never enjoyed, and frankly, never even imagined. While she and Mr. Johnstone disagreed not infrequently, some-times quite widely, he always listened politely, argued intelligently, and conceded defeat as often as she did. He was open to changing his opinions in a way she had never before experienced. It might have seemed suspicious, but there was nothing to be gained by playing games with her. He already had what he wanted: access to the library book. What more could she offer him? So, she resolved to enjoy the unusual experience while she could.

Friday morning, he arrived at his usual time. Mama herself greeted him at the door as though Hill could not be trusted for such an important visitor.

"You are very welcome, Mr. Johnstone, please do

come in." Mama flounced into the parlor where Mary waited. "Might I send some chocolate for you?"

"Thank you, Mrs. Bennet, but I fear I will not be able to make my usual visit today." He bowed slightly.

Mary rose from her place at the window-side table where she always sat whilst waiting for him. "Pray why not?" Hopefully their spirited debate yesterday had not been so spirited as to dis-suade him …

"You must forgive me, but my mother and I return to Heth-erington tomorrow, and there is some business I must see to before we leave." He really did look a bit disappointed, and since he was hardly an accomplished actor, the look was to be believed.

"We will be sorry to lose your company, sir." Mama had a vaguely suggestive note in her tone, but it was entirely unclear what she might be pushing for.

"Likewise, madam. But I do not come bearing only bad news. My mother offers both you ladies an invitation for refresh-ments this afternoon. It seems she is so grateful for the way you have relieved her of my disagreeable companionship that she would like to thank you both personally." There was a little chuckle in his voice. Though he teased his mother mercilessly, and it seemed she could be … ah … difficult … at times, there was a genuine warmth between them that Mary could not help but envy.

"How delightful. We should be glad to attend your moth-er—at the vicarage I assume?"

"Yes, my aunt, Mrs. Daring, is looking forward to your call as well." He glanced toward Mary, one eyebrow lifted in question.

"It has been far too long since we have been able to spend time with her. We will enjoy it very much. Pray excuse me. I must make some arrangements with

Hill for the afternoon." Mama bus-tled off as though on an important errand. But it was obvious that her chore held no real urgency, and she was merely creating what she would have called "an opportunity."

Mr. Johnstone stood, hands limply in front of him, looking at Mary a little sheepishly. "Honestly, I really do have to manage a number of—"

"Pray sir, you have no need to defend yourself to me." She stood and took a few steps closer to him.

"Perhaps not, but I do not want you to misunderstand my abandonment of you this morning. I would much rather study with you than attend to market orders, delivery instructions, and school contracts. So, I would like to extend you an offering of good will."

"An offering? I do not understand." Her brow knit in pre-cisely the way her mother warned her to avoid.

He scuffed his toes on the carpet. "You have never met my mother. She is not exactly as one might expect."

"I definitely do not understand. You have spoken a great deal about her." She tried to catch his gaze.

His head hung down just a mite—much like a guilty little boy. "It is true, I have, but perhaps I have not included all the rele-vant details."

It was hard to tell if he was being playful or not. She al-lowed a hint of sternness into her voice. "Pray tell me what you mean." She folded her arms across her chest.

"In the first place, you may have heard that she is half blind and deaf." He chewed his bottom lip.

"Maria Lucas mentioned that. She thought you were most solicitous of your mother's infirmities."

"I am not surprised." He raked his fingers through his hair. "I do not wish to make my mother seem disingenuous, but she is in full possession of all her faculties."

"Then why…?"

"Why indeed." He cradled his forehead in his hand. "Since my father's death, she finds herself wearied by what she considers unworthy conversations and interactions. And there are increasing-ly many of those."

Mary's eyes widened. "So she feigns incapacity—"

"To avoid what she finds dull or distasteful … which seems to be a great deal lately."

Mary snickered under her breath.

"I am pleased you can find it amusing. My sister and I find it rather embarrassing. I go along with it because trying to cure her of it has been utterly ineffective, and all told there seems little enough harm to it."

She covered her mouth and giggled. "I can well understand. Having sat through my share of social calls which were disagreeable, I can appreciate her strategy for what it is."

"Then you are not put off?"

Oh, the utter astonishment on his face! "Hardly. I can re-spect her resourcefulness."

"And you will keep what I have said between us alone?" His eyes all but pleaded with her.

"Of course. I value your insight and will endeavor my best not to be insipid to her. I fear, though, at times my mother…." Her smile was nearly impossible to suppress.

"My aunt has spoken of Mrs. Bennet often enough that my mother knows what to expect. She will not paint you with the same brush."

"That is most gracious of her, I am sure."

"I hope you shall have an enjoyable afternoon with her." He bowed again. "But I really must leave." His eyes revealed true reluctance.

"I hope all your errands are rewarded with easy success." Mary curtsied.

"Thank you." He disappeared through the parlor door, feet dragging.

What an odd conversation. What kind of woman was Mrs. Johnstone? How much disability would she affect today? It would be an interesting tea, no doubt.

Mama had insisted on having the carriage even though the vicarage was an easy walk—closer than Lucas Lodge. But it was far more impressive to arrive in the coach, so that was the way they would travel. Luckily, the farm could spare the horses, and they were all spared a spirited debate between Mama and Papa. No one was disappointed by that.

Mama prattled on the entire way to the vicarage: about Lydia's recent letter, the latest news from Lady Lucas, and a num-ber of other points of interest that were of little matter to her listen-er. Just as well, Mary had perfected the skill of smiling and nod-ding to feign interest quite some time ago.

Not entirely unlike Mrs. Johnstone.

This should be an interesting afternoon.

Mrs. Daring greeted them at the door. She was a stout, plain woman, the mother of four strapping sons, all currently off at school. Her eyes were pretty and kind though, and she had a sweet voice and laugh that easily made one forget she was plain.

Mrs. Daring led them to the parlor where Mrs. Johnstone was already installed. According to Mama, the room was the right size and properly decorated to be in the home of a vicar: welcom-ing and neat, nei-ther too high nor too low for their station. To Mary, it seemed rather nondescript, bearing little that re-vealed any-thing about the resident. But according to Mama, that was a proper thing. Why, she had no idea, but to question Mama on the matter was probably not wise. The table before Mrs. Johnstone bore a pitcher of lemonade and a plate of still-warm biscuits that smelled of spices and sweetness.

"That you so much for accepting our invitation on such short notice." Mrs. Daring sat next to Mrs. Johnstone. "I pray you did not have to rearrange oth-er plans."

The two women could not have been more differ-ent. Mrs. Daring was plump and blonde and sweet, like an under-baked Chelsea bun with shiny raisin eyes and a disposition that was uni-versally pleasing. Most everyone in the parish liked her very well—which might not sound like a great accomplishment, but indeed it was.

Mrs. Johnstone was dark, her face lined and cross-looking, with sharp angles everywhere. Rather like an overbaked paste crust, she looked like she might go to pieces with little warning. Clearly her son did not fa-vor her. In truth, by appearance alone, she was fairly intimidating.

"Not at all, Mrs. Daring. We are only too happy to come."

"Before we get too comfortable, pray, Mrs. Ben-net, might I trouble you for your assistance with my rose garden?" Mrs. Daring clasped her hands before her ample bosom. "It is well known in Hertfordshire that there is no one who keeps roses as well as you do."

Even Papa conceded that the general opinion was right. Mama's rose beds were a sight to behold.

Mama's cheek's flushed. "You are far too generous. My rose gardens are hardly that impressive, but I would be pleased to help you in any way I can."

"Pray come and see. There is this spot in the back where something is vexing my roses, and I have no notion of what it could be." Mrs. Daring led Mama out, describing her troubled plants as they went.

Mrs. Johnstone turned to stare at Mary. Her eyes were dark, sharp, and clear. A quick intelligence flickered behind them. Defi-nitely not half-blind.

. "We have been enjoying some fine weather, have we not?" It was rarely a mistake to remark about the weather. Mary sat across from Mrs. Johnstone.

"I do not see why you would not do for Mr. Collins." Mrs. Johnstone pressed her lips into a thin, sour frown and leaned slight-ly back in her thinly-upholstered chair.

"Excuse me?" Mary gasped but managed not to allow her jaw to gape—just barely.

"You heard me well enough. That Lady Lucas went on and on about her eldest daughter's conquest with that Collins man." She dug her elbows into the chair's arms to sit up a little straighter.

Mary's cheeks burned. That was not a topic Mrs. Johnstone was welcome to discuss with her.

Her eyes narrowed. "Why would he have chosen a woman ten years older than you when he could have had a young and—reasonably pretty—wife?"

"I … thank you for the compliment…." Not that it actually sounded like one.

"That was not a compliment."

How kind of her to clear up the confusion so

quickly.

"It was merely a statement of fact. You are a decade younger than Mrs. Collins, and you are not displeasing to look at. Not the beauty of your family as I understand—"

"No, that would be my sister Jane. There is hardly one woman in fifty who would not suffer standing beside her." At least it was easy to slip into her script about her elder sisters.

"You must be relieved she is no longer in your house."

"Why would I feel that way?" Why did this woman persist in this line of questioning?

"What plain girl would not appreciate having one less beauty to be compared to?"

"Jane is a sweet and gentle soul who goes out of her way to be pleasing to those around her." It was far easier to say because it was true.

"So you are not jealous of her beauty?" Mrs. Johnstone rested her chin on an open first and stared.

"That is a very personal question."

"The most interesting ones are." Mrs. Johnstone eyebrows flashed up. "So are you jealous?"

Mary's eyes narrowed. "Have you a very pretty sister?"

Mrs. Johnstone laughed thinly. "Interesting that you would think to ask. Suppose I do."

"Then one might wonder if you ask of jealousy as a com-parison to your own experience."

"One might. But that one might also be avoiding a more significant question. Why did you not do for Mr. Collins? Lady Lucas made it sound as though there were those who believed that you would make an excellent match for the man."

"I certainly cannot speak for him and would not begin to. But I believe that his attentions were directed to my second eldest sister, Elizabeth. When he did not succeed with her, I think his dis-appointment might have turned his eyes away from our family circle." There was enough truth in that answer to satisfy anyone, or at least there should be.

"And the former Miss Lucas' behavior had nothing to do with it?" Mrs. Johnstone cocked her head as though she suspected something that none would say in polite company. But then again, was this polite company?

"It sounds as though you want me speak negatively of our friend."

"I am not leading you in any direction, merely asking your opinion."

"I know nothing of her behavior save what I witnessed in public which was always appropriate and ladylike. If you wish to know any more, you will have to consult the lady in question." Mary straightened her spine and pulled her shoulders back.

"So you bear her no ill will?"

Mary licked her lips. "Surely you have heard from your son that I have spent the last two weeks working diligently on a favor for her. Is that the behavior of someone bearing animosity?"

"One never knows. Sometimes people act quite the opposite of how they actually feel."

"I have heard that said." Mary rose—if she stayed seated one more moment she might well lose control over her tongue—and wandered toward the fluttering curtains. "But, if one believes in the hand of Providence, then one must also believe things work out as they should, whether or not one understands what that looks like at any given moment."

"Those are brave words for a young woman who may have watched her only chance at a future wed another."

She completely turned her back on Mrs. Johnstone. Though it might be considered rude, it was also necessary. "Perhaps so. But I am not yet one and twenty. It would be foolish to resign myself to any particular fate just now."

"So you are not bitter?"

"What I feel or think in the privacy of my own thoughts is not for you or anyone else to know. I believe that one reaps what they sow, and that is a choice I can make separate from any of the things you are asking me about. Since you seek to judge me, mad-am, I would ask you to do so on the basis of what I have been seen to do and heard to say, not what others suppose about me." Her breath left little clouds on the window pane that disappeared as quickly as her words.

"That is surprisingly more difficult a favor to receive than you might realize, but an entirely fair one to ask for."

Mary turned to find Mrs. Johnstone pouring glasses of lem-onade. Footfalls and voices filled the corridor outside the parlor.

"I cannot thank you enough, Mrs. Bennet," Mrs. Darning gushed, leaning on Mama's arm. I had no idea the bushes were not enough in the sun. I will move them directly to the spot you sug-gested."

Mama looked ever so satisfied. She did so like to be help-ful. It was good that one of them was pleased with their visit.

For her part, Mrs. Johnstone had returned to playing herself as deaf and blind, smiling and nodding as Mama carried the con-versation. That made it a little easier for Mary to spend the rest of their visit with a woman who surely disliked her.

Saturday morning proved to be one of those mornings not cloudy enough to be called gloomy but not sunny enough to be called cheerful. It was unre-markable, ordinary, average to the point of being a hint dreary. Mary lingered in bed a full hour, arguing the merits of getting up at all. The call of a library book that needed to be returned could not be ig-nored, though. There was no point in wasting her pocket money to pay a fine that need not be incurred. Not to mention her monthly subscription had begun anew and she could acquire a new book. So she forced herself out of bed.

How odd it was not hurrying through her toilette to be ready by the time Mr. Johnstone arrived. It seemed such a normal part of her routine now. Granted, it should be a relief not to be rushing about first thing in the morning. Really, it should. But somehow, it all felt a bit empty and pointless. The draw of sensible conversation and interesting opin-ions had been definitely worth getting up for.

Silly, foolish girl. She had known it would only be a short time from the onset. To miss it now was noth-ing but girlish ridicu-lousness. No, instead she should learn from it. Reflect on the expe-rience and glean from it what she could.

She slipped on her favorite blue spencer and but-toned it. He had once mentioned he liked the color blue, but it had been her favorite long before that. Bonnet in hand, she headed downstairs. Hopefully, no one would be around to notice her. Luckily, the en-tire family seemed determined to sleep in, so she was able to gather her basket and library book and duck out without explaining herself—a luxury indeed.

The morning air had nothing to recommend it—though nothing to really complain about, either. The sun hung where it should, the ground was neither dry and dusty nor wet and muddy, the temperature and the wind were exactly what one might expect at this time of year. It was wholly unremarkable. Exactly what this morning should be: wholly unremarkable.

Except that it was not. She noticed, and resented, every un-remarkable thing about it as it mocked the very remarkable way that she felt. If only she could control her feelings as well as she could control her tongue.

Loneliness was no stranger. No, that sensation was more or less a constant companion, so familiar that it was nearly unnotice-able.

Except for today.

Gracious! She had not even realized how she had grown accustomed to his company. She pressed her palms to her cheeks. Mr. Johnstone's frequent attendance upon Longbourn had been awkward and chafing at first, to be sure, but she had indeed grown accustomed to it.

Was that what Lizzy had meant in her last letter when she had described Mr. Darcy's presence taking on a happy familiarity like a favorite shawl one wore not because she was cold, but rather because it was comforting? She stopped and blinked several times. That phrase had made no sense when she had first read it, but now it was completely clear.

She swallowed hard. Mr. Johnstone was gone and

would not likely return to Meryton anytime soon.

No, that was not the point to dwell upon. She balled her fists and forced her feet into motion. Her boots and skirt swished through the green grass, tugging against them slightly as burrs tried to catch her along the way. The salient point to remember was one might be at ease and comfortable in the company of a man, even one living in the same house. That was an important and significant revelation.

Living at Longbourn one might never have surmised amia-bility in a couple was possible. And though Jane made that claim for herself and Bingley, one could never be certain how much of Jane's positivity should be believed. Firsthand experience with the concept, seeing it for herself, and identifying it for what it was—that was a good thing. And something which very well might change her attitude toward the married state.

Of course that could be a double-edged sword—no, that was not a useful place to go now either. She pressed the heels of her hands to her temples and closed her eyes. She really must con-trol her thoughts.

So, what other advantages might be gleaned from recent events? She chewed her lip. It was not always easy to predict Mr. Johnstone's opinions. Sometimes they differed wildly from what she expected, but in all cases, they were well-thought out and rea-soned. Disagreeing with him was not always—not usually to be entirely honest—a bad thing. He welcomed debate, even on weightier matters which he could simply claim proficiency and dismiss anything she might say. That was unusual in a man—at least in her experience.

Certainly Mr. Collins had not been that way. Her

stomach tightened into a familiar little knot. He expected to be the expert in all things, unless of course Lady Catherine had an opinion, then her expertise surpassed all others. Otherwise, though, he really brooked no disagreement, often ending discussions with platitudes like: "You cannot expect to understand so weighty a matter, Cousin Mary. Women were not formed for such depth of thought."

How often she wanted to remind him Lady Catherine was a woman. But at no time did that sound like a good idea. There seemed to be something of a temper in him, behind the well-practiced smiles and nods he offered. No, it would not do to find out more about that.

Perhaps it really had been for the best that Charlotte had married Mr. Collins instead of herself.

She stopped again. Never, absolutely never had she thought that before. But there it was, as plain as day. She really was better off without Mr. Collins. Her disappointment had been too sharp before to allow the idea room. But in truth, perhaps it was Providence working things out for the best.

Something slipped from her shoulders, a heaviness, a sense of being ill-used, perhaps. Whatever it was, it was gone, and she felt easier for it.

That was certainly a worthwhile revelation.

She pressed on, her steps lighter. The library was one street away now. Had a cloud moved past the sun? Was it just a touch brighter than it had been moments ago? Probably not, that was most likely her heart playing tricks on her mind. But perhaps, this once, she would not challenge it. Who could not do with a brighter and cheerier sort of day?

The library bustled with patrons—Saturday mornings were usually one of the busiest times at Clarke's. Kitty was correct; the loss of the officers there was noticeable. It did take away from some of the novelty of the place and there were certain young la-dies, whom she would not mention by name, who did not seem to visit as frequently since their departure.

Papa had occasionally wondered aloud if their departure was any great loss to the library itself. Realistically, though, it had to be. Those young ladies might not rent books, but they did pur-chase re-freshments and trinkets, so they supported the place with-out even reading.

But Mary was not there for novelty nor the company, nor even refreshments nor trinkets. She would return her book, find another, and be on her way.

She dodged through the crowd to the desk holding the li-brary catalog. What to read now? Charlotte had written to her ask-ing her to hurry and send the notes on The Moral Miscellany and to begin study on another book recommended by Lady Catherine.

Of course, Lady Catherine would have endorsed all the ed-ucational materials they were to use. How else would Mr. Collins ever make a decision? And why else would he have chosen to use a text over thir-ty years old? At least Mr. Johnstone could attribute the choice to something better. A father who prom-ised to send his son to the Hetherington school had specifically requested Mr. Johnstone make some use of it in his teaching. At least that seemed a more solid reason than intimidation by one's patroness.

After a fortnight of dedicated reading and study of material that did not particularly intrigue her, it was difficult to rouse herself to the idea of doing yet another fortnight of the same. Especially when she could not choose the material for herself.

Oh, how the idea chafed today. It had been annoying be-fore, but today, it was nigh on intolerable.

Charlotte could make do with the notes Mary would take to the post today. If she wanted more, then she could do the work herself. No real friend would really insist that Mary do more than she already had.

At least that was how Mr. Johnstone had made her feel. He had suggested that the work she was doing was a great favor and should be appreciated, not expected and treated as though it were nothing.

She brushed off the notion at first; it was easier that way for the idea bore with it some disturbing implications. But perhaps, as in other ways, Mr. Johnstone was right: she did not need to feel obligated to answer to everyone's demands simply because she did not—yet—have a home to manage herself.

The thought coursed through her, shaking her hands and nearly melting her knees. She nearly dropped the library catalog as she sucked in a sharp breath to collect herself. What might she se-lect if she chose for herself alone? She opened the catalog again and scanned page after page. There, yes, that would do nicely.

She returned her book and asked for the first novel off the new acquisitions list, clinging to the counter for support. Thankful-ly, the clerk was quick. She took the novel with trembling hands and all but staggered into the first open chair in the reading room. How fortunate that chair happened to be in a secluded, quiet nook, away from the group of chittering girls and the young men sur-rounding them.

She opened the novel though she could not focus.

Mr. Johnstone had intimated—and he was right—she was more than one to be ordered about, to be expected to do as others insisted. She was not lesser for being unmarried at a time in life when it was perfectly natural to be so. She could choose where she would be-stow her efforts; moreover, it was perfectly right and acceptable to do so.

The page in her lap blurred. She dragged her sleeve across her eyes. Mr. Johnstone would probably enthusiastically entertain her thoughts of the matter if he were here with her. It was easy to imagine his eyes sparkling at the ideas, and his voice encouraging her to consider the matter even more deeply.

If only he were here to do just that.

.

❧Chapter 5

A VERY LONG fortnight passed—it contained only the requi-site fourteen days but somehow felt far longer. On the upside, it gave Mary sufficient time to read and re-read two more novels. How refreshing it was to indulge in something for her pleasure alone and no other reason. Certainly the indulgence could not go on indefinitely. No doubt, soon enough she would crave the stimu-lation of something more substantive, but for now, the extrava-gance was not a bad thing. Or so Mr. Johnstone would have said.

She sighed. Mr. Johnstone. That was the downside.

For the most part, she managed to keep memories of him at bay. Busyness had proved to be her friend. Not only was there much to be done at home, but Mama insisted she accompany her on near-ly all her social calls, and Kitty demanded she walk with her to Meryton every other day. It was not difficult to remain active enough to keep her thoughts controlled.

But Saturday mornings, particularly on her journey to and from the library—as she was doing right now—she permitted her-self the luxury of thinking on him: his tousled visage, which had the unusual effect of growing more pleasant the more time one spent with him; his deep laugh, which he applied liberally to any-thing he found amusing; the peculiar sense of humor that went with it—he found the oddest things funny, truth be told. But that was intriguing in and of itself, trying to suss out exactly where and why he found humor where he did. His persistent way of question-ing her until she finally spilled her musings to him, not taking the typical evasive answers when she attempted to offer them. Unfor-tunately, those thoughts only served to remind her of what she most wanted to avoid dwelling on: that she was lonely without him.

She paused at a dusty stile, looking a mite dejected in the morning sun. Surrounded by green fields and a soft breeze, it should have been quite cheerful. But somehow, the stile's pleasant surroundings could not lift its spirits. A sparse vine tried unsuc-cessfully to wind itself around the lowest beam. It bore only three scraggly leaves and a shriveled flower bud to show for its efforts. Poor withered thing, so little success for so much work.

Surely the vine could not have worked as hard to climb the stile as she had. Why did it feel like so much effort today?

She jumped down from the stile, neatly avoiding a soup-plate sized patch of mud. She turned toward the north and west, peering into the soft, fluffy clouds in the distance. What a shame that Hetherington should be a full ten miles away.

Ten miles was too far away to keep up a steady acquaint-ance with a man to whom she could not even write.

That thought was far more common than any other and harder to keep at bay. Resentment teased at the edges of her soul. Somehow Lizzy managed to have her Mr. Darcy, although he was from very far away. It seemed unfair that the smaller separation between her and Mr. Johnstone should prove insurmountable.

But that resentment was ungracious and ungrateful. Perhaps he only crossed her path as a means by which she might learn different ways of looking at the world and perspectives she might never have encountered otherwise. Not every encounter was meant to be a lasting one. Not every person remained in one's life forever.

Sometimes it seemed too cruel they did not.

Enough! Enough of such thoughts and ramblings. They did nothing to ease her temper or put her in a frame of mind for dealing with Mama and Kitty. Since she could make out Longbourn on the horizon, she needed to find her equanimity quickly. Funny how the house should appear so proper and staid from afar when it proved to be entirely unlike that inside. Perhaps she needed to slow her pace. Given that Mama intended for them to work in the stillroom today, she needed all her faculties focused on tolerating the close quarters and over-management that Mama was apt to provide.

Hill greeted her at the door, her face an utterly neutral mask. That was not a good sign. "Your mother asks that you attend her in the morning room as soon as possible."

Mary nodded and grit her teeth. There was no telling what that could mean. Well, that was not true. It was sure to be some sort of bother, but of what nature, that was the part that could not be predicted. Best not procrastinate. It would only make things more trying.

The rest of the family was gathered around the large round table in the sunny morning room. Papa, seated opposite the win-dow, seemed engrossed in his newspaper, muttering under his breath at something he read. Kitty hunched in a sunbeam, squinting at a piece of white work she had been struggling with all week. She had plucked it apart, what was it—perhaps three times now?—and was attempting the pattern one more time. Mama appeared to ig-nore them all, focused on a slice of ham, slicing it into tiny pieces and pushing them around her plate. How strange, even a little sus-picious.

The smells of breakfast made her stomach grumble—salty, savory ham, warm fresh toast, hints of sweetness from the jam pots. She had not eaten before she left for the library. It was long past time that she did. She slipped into her typical place between Papa and Kitty. Pray Mama might only acknowledge her and ask no questions, make no remarks.

"It is good of you to finally join us." Mama barely glanced up from her plate.

"I always go to the library on Saturday morning." Mary poured herself a cup of coffee, more because it annoyed Mama that she would drink it instead of tea than because she really wanted it at the moment.

"Well, I am sure you will regret having been away so long when you hear the news. Such news that I have for you!" Mama waved a letter.

"Tell us, Mama." Kitty shivered with excitement.

Mary strained to see the moving paper. Her name was on the direction. "Mama! How could you?"

Papa looked up from his newspaper, eyes narrow and lips tight. "There, there, child, you need not be upset. Your good moth-er was only trying to save you the effort necessary to open and read your own mail." He did not approve of Mama's behavior, but when he did nothing to stop her, his disapproval meant little.

"Pray give it to me, Mama. Do you not think it forward of you to read it even before I have?" Mary reached for her letter, nearly knocking over a jam pot. The answer, of course, was that it was not only forward, but also completely improper and wrong. But Mama would never acknowledge that.

Mama pulled it away from her. "With that attitude, I do not know that I should let you have it at all."

"Mama! It is addressed to me, not to you. It is mine. Pray give it to me!" She slammed her hands on the table. Dishes rattled.

"Let her have her letter. Is it not enough that you already know what it contains? Do be good enough to share it with the in-tended recipient before the entire household is upended." Papa's voice had the barest edge to it.

But that was usually all the warning one had before Papa truly lost his temper. It did not happen often—it had been a year since his last real outburst—but when it happened, it was very, very memorable. Waiting another full twelvemonth to experience that again would not be too long to wait.

Mama snorted and flung the letter at Mary. "If you must. It would be much faster if I simply told you what was in it."

"I much prefer to read it myself." Mary sat down and held the letter below the tabletop, away from Kitty's prying eyes. She would have that much privacy at least.

"Do not sit there in silence, girl. You may as well read it to us." Mama patted the table beside her plate like an anxious wood-pecker.

"I will read the relevant points to you once I have finished reading it." Mary did not look up from her letter, but it was easy to imagine Mama's face.

Papa smirked. Kitty giggled under her breath.

Mary focused on the handwriting: thin and spidery, sharp and pointy. From Mrs. Johnstone? Why on earth would she be writing to Mary? It was not as though the matron even liked her, much less wanted her as a correspondent.

Miss Bennet,

I hope this missive finds you in good health. Since our return to Hetherington, my son has begun the undertaking he discussed with you. We have taken six young scholars into our home to be taught by him. (And cared for by me although I do not think he sees it that way.)

I do not know how to put this in a politic fashion, so I will be plain. The children are simply wild and unruly, nothing to what my sons were like as boys. I find I am at my wits end from the moment I rise until I see them to bed each night and hours beyond that. I am quite certain I cannot do this much longer.

I have written to my daughter to come assist me in this en-deavor. But she will not be able to come before the end of the month. Thus, I petition you for your most gracious assistance.

Pray, can you come and help me manage these youngsters until my daughter is available to assist? I am truly at the end of myself and do not know where else to turn. Come whenever you can. Even today would not be too soon.

In desperation,

AJ

"Are you not excited? Is this not wonderful news?" Mama bounced on her chair and clapped much as Kitty might.

"I am not sure how I feel about it." Mary chewed her lip.

It was all so strange. Was Mrs. Johnstone really so desper-ate that she would invite a woman who she disliked to come help? Had she so few connections to call upon in her moment of need? What kind of children were these? The youngest should not be less than seven years old, old enough not to require much in the way of supervision. The situation simply did not make sense.

"I think—" Kitty leaned forward, struggling to get her share of the conversation. "If it were me, I should very much like to go."

"You have been invited to stay with the Johnstones! By Mrs. Johnstone herself. What could be more acceptable and proper than that?" Mama waved her hands instead of shouting.

"Perhaps you and I have not read the same invitation, Ma-ma. It does not seem she wants me as a guest but as some sort of governess for the students they have taken in." One more demand placed upon her because, since she was unmarried, clearly she had nothing better to do with her time. Not even one-

and-twenty and already people treated her as a spin-ster.

"Yes, yes, I saw that, but it hardly signifies. What are a few children around the place?" Mama brushed the notion aside. "What matters is that it will put you in good stead to see and be seen by Mr. Johnstone. What is more, you will be able to show him how clev-er you are at managing a house and the children. What better way—"

Yes, yes, to get herself a husband .... "Pray stop, Mama, just stop." Mary stood and planted her hands hard on the table. "I hardly know what to think, or what I wish to do. I need time to consider—"

Mama's eyes bulged like an angry pug's. "Why do you think there is any question? You will go to Heth-erington as soon as you are packed and the carriage readied. There is no decision to be made."

Mary's shoulders knotted. "Just like when you sent Jane out in the rain to visit Netherfield."

"You see how well that turned out for everyone. A most agreeable outcome. I do not understand why you would object." Mama tossed her head and snort-ed.

"She was dreadfully ill—can you not recognize how dan-gerous—" Mary clutched her forehead.

"But she did get Mr. Bingley," Kitty mumbled, picking at her fingernails.

"I am not sending you out on horseback in the rain, child. Stop complaining. Your papa will see to the coach, and you will have an easy and pleasant journey. It should only take what, two hours to get there?"

"But I do not know if I even want to go." Mary pumped her fists at her sides.

"You are going, and that is the final word on the matter. Now go upstairs and pack, or I will send Kitty and Hill to do it for you." Mama pointed at the door.

Mary planted her feet, trembling.

Papa stood, sighing. "I suppose that is my cue to inform the groom of the plans. Come Mary, I will have your trunk brought down from the attic." He extended a hand toward her.

Just as well, another moment in the morning room and she would say something most untoward especially as Kitty was now muttering about wishing to accompany her.

Papa tucked her hand in the crook of his arm and led her through the shadowy corridor toward the stairs. "Do not let your mother upset you. We all know she only wants to see the best for you."

"Should I not have some say in what that might look like?" Mary dragged her feet along the old carpet. Why was Papa taking such an interest in this?

"Of course you should. But I think it would do you some good to spend time with your friends, out of the reach of your mother's—"

"Interference?"

"Her concern for your welfare."

"Do you know the terms I have been invited for?" She handed him the missive.

He stopped, adjusted his glasses, and read the letter. "Unruly children? Ah, I see your reluctance now. But tell me, how did you find the Gardiner children when last they visited?"

She shrugged. "They were quite well behaved though a bit energetic at times."

"How did your mother describe them?"

Mary paused, her jaw dropping slightly.

"I believe her words were unruly and nigh on in-tolerable except for the efforts you girls made in reining them in. Or do I recall the matter incorrect-ly?" His eyebrows rose high over his glasses.

"I think I enjoyed their visit so much that I did not remem-ber Mama's discomfort."

"Perhaps that is worth consideration." He nudged her to-ward the stairs and turned toward the front door.

She climbed the creaky stairs slowly, deliberately. There was, of course, no guarantee that Mrs. John-stone's tolerance—or rather intolerance—of childishness was the same as Mama's, but it was not unreasonable to assume it might be.

On the other hand, so much about this felt like one more demand placed upon her because she might have nothing better to do. Mr. Johnstone had shown her how sorely tired she was of that.

But … Mama did have a point. It could put her in the way of Mr. Johnstone. And that … that was a pleasant possibility, in-deed.

At the worst, even if Miss Johnstone were delayed, it would be what, three weeks, perhaps a month, that Mrs. Johnstone would need her assistance? Truly, that was not so very long. And if she brought money for a stage coach ticket in case it truly was intolerable, it might be nice to be away from Longbourn for a few weeks.

Mama would find it appalling if she had to ride the stage-coach back home, probably alone, without a servant to accompany her. But hopefully, it would not come to that. And if it did, she would deal with it when it happened.

Mary trotted up the last few steps. She would need

several aprons and a warm shawl….

All told, it was a good thing Mary was able to pack quickly and act decisively even amidst Mama's flurries and Kitty's jealous whining. How she stomped around Mary's room proclaiming that she should be allowed to go as well—after all, it was not proper for Mary to travel alone. Besides, it was not fair that she never got asked to go anywhere ….

Mary dragged her hand down her face. The effort required not to respond to that latter remark should have earned her a knighthood. She patiently explained not once, but three times that since Kitty had never even met Mrs. Johnstone, she had little busi-ness imposing on the Johnstones with a visit. She might as well not have tried to be patient for all the good it produced.

Kitty fell onto Mary's bed in a paroxysm of tears. Not that any of them appeared to be real, to be sure. She stormed up and down the corridor outside their rooms, declaring the unfairness of life, especially her own.

Lydia would have been impressed with the amount of cha-os that ensued. Mama was on the verge of insisting that Kitty be allowed to go when Papa stepped in to announce the carriage was ready. He noted if there were any delay, the driver would not be able to return before dark tonight, and Mama's plans to use the coach for calls tomorrow would be for naught.

Had he intended to thwart Kitty and Mama, or had the tim-ing been coincidental? With Papa, it was diffi-cult to tell. But for now, she would assume he was trying to help her in his own pecu-liar sort of way. It felt better to think thusly.

The carriage was loaded, and Papa handed her aboard, all without distracting Mama or Kitty as they comforted one another over Kitty's loss.

And no one seemed to notice.

When Jane and Lizzy and Lydia had departed, there was great crying and flurries at how they would be missed. Even when Lizzy left to visit Charlotte, Mama had made the most of the op-portunity to dote and be attentive to her departing daughter. In some ways, it was nice to avoid all that uncomfortable at-tention. But on the other hand, it was cold and lonely and sad.

If she dwelt on her departure, she would put her-self in such a state that she would be no fit company when she arrived at Ash-lea Cottage, the vicarage at Hetherington Parish. Since Mrs. John-stone's disposi-tion was uncertain at best, and there was no telling the true nature of the students, she needed all her facul-ties in prop-er order. Best set all that aside and concentrate on her destination.

After several minutes of trial and error, she found the most comfortable spot in the carriage—on the far seat, near the right hand side glass, where she never got to sit when she rode with her family—and settled in for the duration. The leather that covered the lumpy squabs was cracked in places now, and the coach springs were definitely worn, but all in all, the luxury of space and quiet proved quite tolerable in-deed.

Ten miles of good road provided a surprisingly restful sort of journey. So much so, the driver's call that they were approach-ing the cottage startled her from her repose. She leaned against the side wall and peeked through the side glass.

Usually, the vicarage of a small country parish was smallish and unpretentious. Draped in vines and roses, Ashlea Cottage was much larger than she had expected. Not pretentious, but certainly noticeable against the backdrop of green fields. There was something peaceful and sweet about the place, like the scent of roses in the sun; picturesque and serene.

Four, no six boys, probably between the ages of eight and eleven, ran back and forth across the front of the house, screaming and laughing. At least for now, it was the happy sort of sound that good natured children made, not the shrill one that tended to ac-company undesirable mischief. Odd, even they did not disturb the serenity of the scene; if anything, they added a touch of whimsy.

Mrs. Johnstone trundled out of the house to meet the coach as it stopped near the front door. The apron tied tight around her middle was stained and limp. Even her mobcap looked tired. The lines in her face seemed deeper than before, and her sharp edges dulled.

The boys ran toward her, circling around her as though she were an obstacle in their game of tag, not unlike the Gardiner boys did when absorbed in their games. She dodged and winced with each shout.

"Miss Bennet! I am so glad you are come. Boys! Boys! Come around and meet my friend Miss Bennet. She will be staying with us. You are to listen to her and obey her." She spoke the last few words with particular clarity and emphasis.

"What is she, some sort of governess?" The tallest, probably the eldest boy, nearly Mary's height, stopped in front of her and looked her straight in the eye.

Her eldest nephew had tried the same tone with

her … once.

Mary folded her arms over her chest. "Young man, I will not be addressed in the third person when I am standing right in front of you. We have been introduced; you shall address your questions to me. I expect you to behave with proper respect and courtesy to all your elders."

He jerked back and blinked at her, a shock of unruly blond hair falling into sharp hazel eyes. "Why should I listen to you?"

"Do you really want me to show you?" She planted her fists on her hips and glared at him.

He opened his mouth, eyes fixed on hers. She narrowed hers just a mite and pulled her shoulders back. He drew a deep breath. She cocked her eyebrow high, allowing pronounced fur-rows to form on her forehead.

He shrank back and bowed his head. "No, miss."

"Then go off and finish your game. I imagine dinner will be served soon. I expect you to be washed up and properly attired for your evening meal. If you are late, do not expect to be seated at all. Is that understood?" She looked at each youngster in turn. "At din-ner you will tell me about yourself and your family so that I may get to know you better."

"Yes, miss." Several of them gulped as they spoke.

On the whole, they did not appear to be bad or unruly chil-dren. Just children with all the energy boys of that age usually pos-sessed. "Off you go then." She gestured a dismissal.

The smallest boy, so blond his hair was nearly white with freckles coating his cheeks, lingered a moment and grabbed her around the knees. She patted his back gently, and he dashed off to catch up with his mates.

"I have not gotten that child to speak three words together to me. I do not know how you managed that." Mrs. Johnstone shook her head and clucked her tongue. "I knew it. I simply knew you would be able to take those boys in hand and set things to right."

Mary turned to watch the children playing. "I appreciate your invitation. I am curious, though, how you would come to that conclusion. Considering I have no young children in my home."

"Some things one just knows." The wry, knowing smile she wore seemed to hide more than it revealed. "Pray, come inside. I will show you to your room." She waved to the driver and spoke a little louder. "Your man can take your trunks up and rest a spell in the kitchen. I imagine the carriage will be wanted back at Long-bourn yet tonight?"

"That is my understanding."

"Tell the cook to set you up with a meal before you are off again." Mrs. Johnstone turned back toward Mary. "Percy is in his bookroom, attending to a few matters of business. He says the boys need time to run about and gives them a free hour before dinner to do so."

"I am sure that makes evening lessons easier for them all."

Mrs. Johnstone shrugged. "If you say so. He is not the one who has to listen to the terrible racket they create." She led Mary inside.

The doorway was a touch short—not that it bothered Mary, but particularly on the left hand side, it might be a bit too low for Mr. Johnstone's comfort. The rest of the house seemed to be equal-ly off. All the walls seemed a bit off plumb, and none of the cor-ners appeared perfectly square. Not so much as to call the struc-ture's soundness into question, but just enough that it had a rather fanciful quality about it. This was the sort of place fairy tales were set in— although it was silly and sentimental to think so.

She peered down the dim hall. The staircase was barely wide enough that small pieces of furniture could be brought up-stairs, but anything large would have been challenging at best. The stairs, though, were regular and even which was a good sign for Mrs. Johnstone's health and welfare. The boys must make a terrible racket tearing up and down the staircase, though.

A door she had not noticed before flung open, nearly into Mary's face. She jumped back.

"Mother, I was just thinking …." Mr. Johnstone stumbled into the corridor and stopped short, staring.

He looked surprised. Very, very surprised. Unex-pectedly surprised. "Mother?"

"Oh, did I fail to mention? I am sure I told you. I asked Miss Bennet to come." She blinked up inno-cently.

"As a matter of fact, you never mentioned it at all."

"I am such a goose. You know how my memory can be at my age." She brushed away his concern with a flick of her hand.

He frowned and tapped his foot. "You never for-get any-thing, Mother."

"Do not exaggerate, Son." Her voice took on the barest edge.

"Unless it is convenient that you should."

"You are being rude." Mrs. Johnstone crossed her arms over her chest and tapped her foot in time with his. "And forgetful."

It was never a good sign when any woman, particularly one's mother, did that.

He seemed undaunted. "And I have been uninformed. Do you not think it would have behooved both of us for you to at least inform me, if not consult me, as to your plans?"

"This is not something one discusses in front of a guest." She pointed into the open study door and stomped through. "Come, now."

Even Mary cringed at the order. They disappeared into the room.

At least they were speaking in hushed tones that she could not make out. That was something. As awkward as this was, hear-ing it all would be much more so.

A lonely hall chair, one that seemed positioned to say "we have hall chairs" rather than to be decorative or useful, beckoned to her. She sank into it since she had not actually been invited into the parlor or any other part of the house.

Yes, that was silly and a technicality, but it felt less obtru-sive sitting in the shadowy hall waiting for them, especially after the sort of greeting as Mr. Johnstone had offered. The carved wooden chair lacked any sort of upholstery, rendering it hard and uneasy. Moreover, it proved several inches too short for her to sit comfortably. The dark corridor all but whispered she was unwel-come.

Was he really so surprised at her arrival? Every expression of his face suggested that he was. Totally and completely sur-prised. But why?

Why would Mrs. Johnstone not have told him of her invita-tion? Heavens, why would she not have consulted with him first? It would only have been proper. Was she afraid that Mr. Johnstone would not have approved of Mary's company?

Her face grew cold, and a familiar knot tightened in her belly. Was it possible that he did not like her as much as she had thought?

She swallowed a sour taste at the back of her tongue. Real-ly, it would not be so surprising if that were the case. It seemed to happen often enough—people never liked her as much as they did the rest of her family. It was not as though she were like Jane or Lizzy or Lydia—she had never been the particularly likeable sort. People usually tolerated her but did not go out of their way to in-vite her, except as a neces-sary courtesy when they did not want to appear uncivil. Even Charlotte, who was ostensibly her friend, only acted truly friendly when she wanted a favor.

Mary wrapped her hands around her waist and pulled them in tight. Was that what all this was about? It seemed Mrs. John-stone was in need of a favor, and Mary was just the most conven-ient person to ask. The ruse of hospitality was only a means by which the favor might appear more civil to ask?

It was not too late to leave now, for the coach was still here, and she could be back at home yet tonight. It would be awful to explain to Mama, but perhaps—yes, that was the best thing. It would not do to im-pose upon Mr. Johnstone. And she did not want to be imposed upon herself. She rose and dusted off her skirt. It should not be too difficult to find the kitch-en....

The door flew open and slapped the wall behind it. Mrs. Johnstone led her son out. She appeared as though nothing unto-ward had happened. On the other hand, if anything, he appeared a little sheepish and a great deal uncomfortable and awkward.

Mary looked away. She was right. He did not like her and was discomposed by her presence. She bit her lip and swallowed hard.

"Pray, forgive me, Miss Bennet. I have been a little ab-sentminded recently. Perhaps my mother is right. The children have addled my brain. I think I may have underestimated the demands of being a school-master." He rubbed his chin and glanced at his mother who elbowed him in the ribs. "She was so kind as to show me in my own journal this was the day she had expected you to arrive. The mistake is entirely mine. I am most heartily sorry. The boys have provided me so many surprises in the last fortnight. I fear that I am not responding well to the unex-pected." He bowed from the shoulders.

She studied him. He was decidedly uneasy, but that did not necessarily mean he was lying. Embarrass-ment could produce the same effect, and if he were embarrassed, then it suggested he had indeed been mistaken. It did not guarantee it by any means, but the possibility was there. Perhaps she should ask to see his journal ….

Mrs. Johnstone cleared her throat and gestured toward the stairs. "Pray, allow me to show you up-stairs and give you a few minutes of peace before dinner when our little band of miscre-ants—"

"Mother, please!"

She snorted. "Young men? Is that more satisfacto-ry? Be-fore they pour in, expecting to be fed and cared for."

Mary glanced through the window—her carriage

had not yet left.

"You handled them so brilliantly upon your first meeting, Miss Bennet. I know you will have them well in hand in only a few days. I so desperately need the help. I know it is a great deal to ask of you, but it is only until my daughter arrives. I would not trouble you except that I have no one else I can call upon." She sighed and everything that might resemble pretense seemed to fall away to reveal a nugget of true distress. "I have no way to repay you except for my deepest thanks for your favor."

Tempting though it was to call for the carriage, it was even more difficult to turn her back on a soul who truly needed assis-tance. And there was the matter of the children who would proba-bly suffer without her help as well. The littlest one seemed a dear child.

She sighed, but only a little. "At what time do you serve dinner?"

Was she imagining things, or was that a smile creeping up Mr. Johnstone's lips?

Chapter 6

SHORTLY AFTER SUNRISE, the children in the rooms above Mary's began to stir. No sound came from the room beside hers, Mrs. Johnstone's chamber. The matron had a fretful night, with sounds of nightmares and walking the creaky floor filtering through the walls the majority of the nighttime hours. The sighs and groans that accompanied her steps were hardly affectations—Longbourn had taught her what those sounded like. No, Mrs. John-stone was experiencing something disturbingly real.

Perhaps she suffered with some kind of digestive com-plaint. It was difficult to tell from the sounds alone, but there might be some way to improve the old woman's comfort. For now though, it would be best to let her sleep.

Mary dressed quickly and made her way upstairs. A maid paced the halls, as if trying to work up the courage to enter the children's rooms. Silly child—but in truth the maid was little more than a child herself, only two, maybe three years older than the oldest of the students. No wonder she was apprehensive.

"Where is Mr. Johnstone?" Mary asked.

The maid wrung her hands in her apron. "He was called away early this morning. It seems there was some emergency—the parish is fond of him, you see. They call on him at all hours with all manner of complaints. Sometimes it is most unnecessary, I think. But today I understand someone was close to dying, and he was wanted very much."

"I see." Well, that would complicate matters quite nicely, now, would it not?

The reason for his absence made it difficult to object. In truth, it was admirable that he was the sort of vicar people counted upon in trouble. There were not many like that, really. Certainly, Mr. Collins was not that type of man. Somehow it was reassuring Mr. Johnstone was.

Still though, if this sort of thing were apt to happen, he real-ly should have some manner of plan in place to deal with it and not leave things to fall as they would. No wonder Mrs. Johnstone needed help. "What do the boys usually do in the morning?"

The girl scuffed her foot along the carpet. "I cannot be en-tirely sure, Miss, but I think he takes them into the schoolroom for some kind of reading or lesson before breakfast."

Well, that would not work. Without knowing specifically their planned lessons, she dared not try to take teaching them upon herself. Asking the boys about their lessons was to invite them to play tricks upon her which no one should have to deal with upon first rising in the morning. Not to mention, it would give them the upper hand, and it was far too early in their relationship to risk that happening.

Mary brushed her hands together and straightened her apron. "Help me get them dressed, then inform the cook I shall have them back at ten o'clock for breakfast. If Mrs. Johnstone should wake while I am out, tell her I have them well in hand and she need only appear below stairs if that is her preference. I would suggest she have a tray in her room this morning and rest as much as she can instead."

The young maid, wide-eyed and a little awestruck, curtsied. "Yes, miss."

Was a small demonstration of decisiveness and action really so worthy of admiration? The thought was a bit unsettling.

"Now for the youngsters." Mary rapped on the door to the first of the rooms and swung it open. Good, it was the three older lads. "Up, up, up. You are to be dressed and waiting for me outside the kitchen in a quarter hour. No time to waste!"

The boys' beds took up almost all the floor space in the awkward little chamber. A crooked press stood near the window, several drawers half open. Several shirts lay on the floor among the socks and shoes. Tidiness needed to be on her teaching plan if not Mr. Johnstone's.

"What about our lessons?" Ah yes, her dear little challeng-er, he would find something to balk at, even if it meant demanding lessons when there were none. Dear young man. "Mr. Johnstone has been called away, so I am taking you out for the morning."

He snorted a disrespectful little sound—the sort of sound that required immediate and unforgettable attention.

"Very well, if you do not wish to join us, you do not have to. I will have the man meet you outside, and you will chop wood this morning." She kept her voice pleasant and level.

He pulled himself upright, as dignified as one might be in only a nightshirt. "Excuse me! I am a gentleman's son. I do not do chores."

The other two boys tittered behind their hands.

"Then your father has been sorely lax in his duty to you. No gentlemen should be unable to do a task that he requires of an-other. Are you saying you are too weak to wield an ax?"

"I am not too weak to do anything." He stamped his bare foot for emphasis.

"Excellent. Then you will be chopping firewood this morn-ing until breakfast."

"Excuse me, miss. What shall the rest of us be do-ing?" The brown-haired, brown-eyed boy asked, rubbing the sleep from his eyes.

"We shall be walking the grounds and examining the flora and fauna we find. Now get yourselves ready." She nodded sharply and closed the door behind her.

The younger boys were less talkative but more in need of assistance getting dressed. Nearly a quarter of an hour passed be-fore she and the maid gathered them up and led them outside the kitchen. The air was still cool and dewy in the shadow of the cot-tage, ideal conditions for a brisk morning walk. They whispered among themselves, reveling in the novelty of the situation.

Mary chewed her lip. Hopefully, she was making the right choices.

The older boys tumbled out from the kitchen door, with just enough pushing and shoving to demonstrate their energies as the longcase clock struck the quarter hour.

The maid rushed to fetch the man who soon ambled along behind her. The gap-toothed grin he tried to hide suggested that particular young man had been a thorn in his side before.

Mary pointed to the oldest boy. "Charles."

"Mr. Mullen." He stuck out his chest.

Now was not the time to roll her eyes.

The younger boys snickered. "We call him Charlie."

He turned on them with a snarl. "She may call me Mr. Mul-len."

"No, if anything you are master, not mister, and even that you have not earned." She balanced her hands on her hips.

A gasp washed across her audience.

His lip curled back, and he pointed at the young maid. "She calls me—"

"Do not think you are above me, for you are not. My father is master of his own estate. If you wish to be called Master Mullen, you will earn the privilege by behaving like a gentleman which I have yet to observe." She turned to the man. "Take Charlie to the wood pile and have him chop firewood until breakfast."

"I am no servant. I will not." He folded his arms over his chest and stomped both feet.

She strode toward him with slow measured steps and stopped a foot from him. "You will do what you are told. You will chop wood. The only question is whether you will do it without being caned."

Behind her, the boys gasped.

"You would not dare. You cannot. You are a woman." His voice was full of bravado, but one eye twitched.

"What has that to do with anything? I have been given charge of you. That is all that need concern you." She smiled with just the corner of her lips—an expression not intended to express pleasure.

"You would not dare. I am bigger than you." Charlie rose to tiptoes to prove the fact.

Mary glanced at the man servant. "I am sure he would be willing to assist me."

"Indeed I am, miss. He's been asking for it for a week full. It'd be my pleasure." He bounced his fist off his other palm, the slapping sounds a touch menacing.

"I shall give you one last chance to choose. Would you pre-fer to chop wood with or without the cane?"

Charlie snorted and stomped and muttered something that sounded like "without" under his breath. The man grabbed him by the arm and half-led, half-dragged him toward the woodpile.

"Did you really mean it, miss?" The older, brown-haired boy's eyes were wide, maybe even a little frightened.

She crouched to his eye level. "I always say what I mean and mean what I say. Do not ever mistake that. I would like to avoid such a to-do again. But do not ever try me. You will find it is a very bad idea."

He gulped and nodded. "My name is Thomas and that—" he pointed to the little blond, freckled boy, "is my brother Nate."

The rest crowded around her and introduced themselves again: David, Richard, and Alexander—all as polite and gentle-manly as they could muster. They had done so at dinner last night, but perhaps this whole incident had driven that from their minds. No need to remind them of that. They were motivated to good be-havior now, and it should be rewarded.

"Excellent. Now that we all know each other, we shall begin our walk." She dismissed the maid and led the boys toward the fields.

Without Charles, the group's demeanor seemed to change. They were pleasant, curious, and energetic, tumbling over each other with questions about everything they saw around them in the fields and woods. Many of those inquiries she could answer, but some she promised they would look up later in the day in the books from Mr. Johnstone's library.

Hopefully he had the necessary books, otherwise—well, she would sort that matter out then.

"Look! I see Mr. Johnstone." David's red hair bounced as he pointed to a tall figure striding up the road.

All the children ran for him, talking over each other trying to be the first to tell him the wonder of what had happened that morning. He stopped, marshalled them into a semblance of order, and heard the story out. Mary stood at a distance, listening and watching his reactions.

When the boys had finished, Mr. Johnstone instructed them to gather all the different leaves they could find. They would work on identifying them during their lessons after breakfast. At his dismissal, they dashed off like a pack of puppies turned loose in a field. Finally, Mr. Johnstone approached her, an odd question on his face.

Mary looked past him, not at him. "Your mother had a rest-less and difficult night last night. I wanted to let her rest this morn-ing."

He nodded, chewing his lower lip. "The local apothecary has been unable to offer her any relief. I am working to have a sur-geon see her."

"Have you a copy of Buchan's Domestic Medicine? I might be able to find some help for her there."

He looked aside. "I inherited the library from an uncle not very long ago. I am rather embarrassed to say, I do not know the extent of it. But consider yourself welcome to any of it you wish to use."

"And catalogue it in the process, I expect?" She cocked her head.

His eyebrows drew together. "I would not think to impose upon you so. The fact you are here and already a great help to my mother is more than I can thank you for."

Her cheeks burned as she ducked her face away.

"Forgive me." He gestured for them to walk. It would not be wise to linger too long out here and not be at the vicarage when the boys returned. "It was brutish of me to forget my mother had invited you to visit with us. I can only imagine how it must have appeared to you yesterday." He scuffed his toes into the dirt as he walked.

"I have been met with more conventional greetings, I must say." She scanned the horizon for the children—it was far easier than looking at him.

He laughed, that deep warm laugh, the one she had been sorely missing. "You are incredibly gracious, Miss Bennet. Here I deserve a sound tongue lashing, and yet you only hint at the severi-ty of my transgression."

"Sometimes it is best to leave as much as possible to the imagination." She sneaked a tiny glance at him.

"It is an interesting strategy." He stepped a little closer to her so their shoulders almost touched as they walked. "The boys seem impressed by the way you have managed Charlie."

"There is a great deal yet to be seen." She shook her head and chewed the inside of her cheek. "I have found it is best in these cases to quickly establish oneself in charge. My aunt has several sons. One fancies himself the master of the house, second only to his father. It requires a strong hand to manage him."

"It would seem you have learned the lesson well."

"That sort of victory is not won in a single day. I have no doubt young Charles will continue to challenge me for some time to come."

"No doubt. Still though, my mother has truly been at her wits end with him. He is the one who drove her to write to you—I was not comfortable imposing upon you so, but she was so desper-ate and so certain you would be able to come and make things right. I do not know how to thank you. It was no small thing to ask of you." He caught her gaze so powerfully she could not turn away.

Had anyone ever said such a thing to her—especially when so deeply felt? It was strange and rather wonderful if she allowed herself to dwell on it. Perhaps she should not. It seemed ephemeral and a little dangerous.

"Would you tell me more about the boys and about your school day and plans for instruction? I think I will be better able to help you if I know more about what you are doing."

"Yes, of course, that is wise." He smiled that gentle ap-proving smile he had and offered her his arm.

Yes, the decision she had made to stay had been a good one.

A fortnight flew past with the household falling into an easy rhythm that emerged out of the initial disarray. It had felt forward to intrude so, but both Johnstones seemed to want—at times even relished—her advice. While they did not take every one of her suggestions—that would have been uncomfortable in and of itself—they did listen and implement the recommendations she felt most strongly about.

In even this short time, the boys seemed calmer, for lack of a better way to describe it. They maintained all the boyish energy children of their age were apt to have, but it felt better focused and more manageable. And when it was not, well, the wood rack out-side was well-filled now.

Thankfully, they had never driven her to the point of using a cane. The boys would face enough of that sort of thing when they entered public school. Was it really necessary to begin now? Could she bring herself to do that if pushed to it? Hopefully they would not drive her to the point when they would all find out.

After breakfast, Mr. Johnstone took his scholars to the schoolroom and Mary and Mrs. Johnstone sat in the morning room over tea and toast, going over the menus and market list for the coming week. Feeding so many ravenous boys required more care-ful planning than meals at Longbourn ever had. Heavens, it was difficult to believe how much they could eat and still claim to be hungry! A good, solid pudding and plenty of potatoes were indis-pensable at every meal. Thankfully, the budget provided enough—barely enough—to accomplish their goals.

The maid almost tripped as she dashed into the morning room, breathless and perturbed.

"Madam?" She curtsied through her stumble. "Were you expecting callers this morning?"

"No, did they give you a card?" Mrs. Johnstone handed her list to Mary.

"No, they said their boy is here. Mullen was their name."

"Oh, gracious, the Mullens! They had written to us and said they would be calling, but I am entirely certain they did not give a date!" Mrs. Johnstone jumped to her feet.

Mary's heart thundered against her ribs. If Charles gave his parents a bad report, how might that reflect upon the school and the Johnstones?

"They wish to see their boy. Immediately, they said. They do not appear to be the kind who will be very patient." The maid wrung her hands in her apron.

"Show them to the parlor, and I will get the child." Mrs. Johnstone glanced at Mary. "I will manage this. You need not wor-ry about greeting company." The statement sounded more like an order than a sugges-tion. She hurried off after the maid.

Pretty sunshine and a delicate, fresh breeze did nothing to suit the ominous mood that descended with Mrs. Johnstone's de-parture. Mary rose and paced between the table and window, dodging the fluttering curtains. The room was only large enough to permit a few steps before she had to turn around and go in the oth-er direction—hardly a satisfying way to work off her nervous en-ergies.

What sort of parents were these, coming all the way to see their child so soon after school had start-ed? That alone was odd. Unless there were illness or some other calamity to befall the es-tablishment, the expense and inconvenience would make visiting in-opportune at the least.

Charles was a handful, to be sure, but he did not seem a spiteful child. Still, if he should see the means by which to gain the upper-hand in the matter, he would probably not be slow on seizing it. What kind of trouble could he cause for the entire estab-lishment? If his parents knew the other students' par-ents, he could poison them all with a few well-chosen words.

She squeezed her eyes shut and clutched her fore-head.

How dreadfully unfair! Mr. Johnstone was an ex-cellent, caring schoolmaster, born to teach. As much as a man could be born to a specific task, he was. He might lose it all, and it could easily be her fault.

A soft scratching at the door caught her attention. What was little Nate doing there? Poor child, his eyes were wide and his face a little pale.

She rushed to him and grabbed his hand. "What is wrong?"

"His parents are here. He told us he would say horrible things about you and make sure you were sent away." Nate's eyes brimmed with tears. "He can-not do that, can he?"

She crouched beside him. "I am not here at his parents' be-hest, but at Mrs. Johnstone's. She is the only one who can ask me to leave."

"But Charlie's parents, he says they are very rich and can do anything they please. He said he could even see that our school is closed because he is treat-ed like a servant and made to chop wood." He clutched her fingers. "I like it here. I do not want to go to another school. Please, do something. You can do anything. I know you can." His eyes pleaded.

"It is not my place. I cannot barge into a conversa-tion among people to whom I have not been introduced. It is just not done. It would look even worse than anything Charlie might have said. It would prove any negative thing he says about us."

"But it is not fair that he should be able to say whatever he wants even if it is not true."

"Untrue things are said all the time. That is why one's con-duct and character must be able to stand and speak for itself even when one cannot." She straightened the lapels of his jacket.

"Is that why you are always going on and on about gentle-manly behavior?"

This was not the time to laugh. "That is one of the reasons."

His features formed into a dear, thoughtful little expression as he stared at his hands. "I shall have to think about that."

"When you have, do come and talk to me about what you have thought."

He peeked up at her. "Are you certain you cannot do something?"

"Very certain. Pray do not fret; it will all be well." She pat-ted his back. "Now, I am sure you will be wanted back in the school room. Go on before you get yourself into trouble."

"Yes, miss." He nodded sadly and dragged his feet as he trudged to the schoolroom.

She glanced toward the parlor. It was tempting to go to the door and try to listen to what was being said. But no, it went against everything she was trying to teach the boys. If she could not be an example to them, she had no place trying to tell them how to behave in the first place.

Perhaps she should get ready to call upon Mr. Johnstone's patron this morning. She and Mrs. Johnstone had been invited to the manor for refreshments with Mrs. Lawson. It would not do to be late. If nothing else, it would be a fitting distraction from what was going on in the parlor. The knots in her stomach tightened as she forced herself upstairs.

Following Mrs. Johnstone's lead, she walked two miles to Leighton Manor. Why did the weather have to be so disagreeably cheery when she felt so turbulent? Worse still, Mrs. Johnstone re-fused to comment on what had taken place in the parlor. It was as if the whole thing had never happened. In the face of such denial, Mary could not even muster the wherewithal to make any other conversation. They traversed the pleasant fields in silence.

The manor and the estate seemed about twice the size as Longbourn, at least, and far more picturesque. It was probably a trick of the season and favorable lighting, but the manor house re-sembled something out of a painting, perched on a little hill and surrounded by green fields and sheep. Perhaps, when she got back to Longbourn, she might try her hand at rendering it in watercolors.

Mary hurried to keep up with Mrs. Johnstone. Not surpris-ingly, she proved quite spry when she wanted to be—and some-thing about this engagement made her want to be very spry today. But why? Even if she asked, Mary would not likely receive an an-swer to that question, either. Though they had become closer over the last few weeks, Mary was in no position to demand intelligence from her hostess.

The Johnstones had always spoken well of their patron, but hardly in the way Mr. Collins spoke of Lady Catherine. Mr. John-stone was no sycophant. There was some sort of distant family connection be-tween the Johnstones and the Lawsons which was only to be expected. That was usually the case when a preferment was granted. It made for a cordial, but not overly sentimental, rela-tionship between the manor and the vicarage.

A butler met them at the carved oak front door, and he led them directly to Mrs. Lawson's parlor. Mrs. Johnstone called it the "ladies' parlor" as, appar-ently, Mrs. Lawson used it exclusively to entertain her personal guests.

If the room reflected their hostess, then she was light, bright, sparkling, and a bit frivolous and flighty. Her choice in fur-nishings seemed a might impracti-cal—a few too many shelves bearing bric-a-brac that appeared to have come from the continent. No books were to be seen in the room at all. The chairs bore intri-cate carvings but hardly looked comfortable, and were set at awk-ward angles which showed off their artistry but would make con-versation more difficult. Odd what furnishings could suggest about a person.

"Mrs. Johnstone, it is so good of you to come. Pray intro-duce me to your young friend." Mrs. Lawson rose from her seat in the middle of the couch backlit by the large window facing a flow-er garden.

Her voice was kind and sweet, maybe a little too much, but just a little. Blonde curls peeked from beneath a lovely lace mobcap with many ribbons and much embroidery to decorate it. Her blue eyes were a fraction too wide-set to give her a look of intelligence. She did not look stupid, by any means, but a mite vacant, perhaps. Was that a trick of her appearance or an actual reflection of her intellect? Perhaps their conversation would reveal that.

Mrs. Johnstone curtsied and gestured toward Mary. "We appreciate your gracious invitation. This is my friend, Miss Bennet. Her father holds Longbourn estate near Meryton."

Mary curtsied.

Mrs. Lawson paused a moment as though she were trying to look up Longbourn on a map. Finally she nodded. "I believe we have ridden past there on the way into town. Yes, yes, I believe we have. You have a pretty wilderness to the side of the house?"

It seemed Mrs. Lawson was a modicum more clever—or at least had a better memory—than she looked. "It has been called that at times, I think. I am rather fond of it as an excellent place to walk."

"One should always have a good place for a walk nearby. I think it is an essential thing for one's soul. Pray, sit down." Mrs. Lawson pointed at several emp-ty chairs near the couch.

The chairs were every bit as uncomfortable as Mary had expected.

"So, Miss Bennet, how do you like our little part of the county?" Mrs. Lawson poured some sort of water containing a sprig of green from a crystal pitcher. It smelt fresh and herbal. Chervil perhaps?

"Very well, indeed. I do not mean to sound overly romanti-cal or sentimental, but it is entirely pictur-esque. Every time I look out the windows, I wonder if I am gazing on a painting." It was pleasant to gush so honestly.

"I must agree. Roses in particular seem fond of our soil. They seem to grow with almost no attention at all." Mrs. Lawson handed her a crystal glass and appeared quite satisfied with Mary's sentiments.

"My mother is known for her roses. She has a way with them, I am told. I think she would find the vil-lage here pleasing indeed. It might inspire a new garden if I know her as well as I think I do." Mary sipped the refreshing, lightly-sweet beverage. It was something Lizzy would have liked.

"It is hard to find a flower that is more regal, more fair than a rose, I think." Mrs. Lawson sighed a little absently.

"The newest issue of A Lady's Magazine has the loveliest pattern for roses on an evening dress, stitched right around the bot-tom of the skirt, with ribbons and puffs. Have you seen it?" It was a little odd for Mrs. Johnstone to reference something that was clearly not to her tastes. She preferred everything simple and una-dorned. Let the materials and work-manship show for themselves, she said, not covered up with fancy bits and bobs.

"I have not. I will definitely—"

The parlor door sailed open, and a brown-haired bundle of spite and fury flew in, her rust-colored skirts swished wildly. "The audacity! The gall! I am utterly beside myself; I cannot imagine."

Mrs. Mullen. It had to be.

She stopped short and stared at Mrs. Johnstone. "What is she doing here?" Was that foam forming at the corner of her mouth?

"Whatever do you mean, cousin? Calm yourself. Please sit down." Mrs. Lawson beckoned her in as though nothing notewor-thy were transpiring.

"You, you are responsible for this outrage!" Mrs. Mullen stood rooted where she was and pointed at Mrs. Johnstone.

"Excuse me, I do not know of what you speak." Mrs. John-stone pressed her hand to her bosom, eyes wide. She might have been mistaken for astonished, but Mary knew better.

"My son! We sent our son to your school under good au-thority that he would be well-looked after and educated. You have turned him into nothing but a servant!" She threw her hands in the air and stormed closer.

"I do not know what you are talking about." Mrs. Johnstone frowned and huffed, her chest puffed out a mite.

The two women resembled nothing so much as two hens about to do battle. It might be laughable if those encounters were not potentially deadly.

"You mean you are not aware that he has been chopping wood outside instead of attending to the lessons we have paid for him to have?" Mrs. Mullen perched her hands on her fists, becom-ing as "big" as possible. A rusty-colored hen for sure.

"Excuse me, Mrs. Mullen," Mary sucked in a deep breath as she stood. "But that is hardly the case. He is in the schoolroom whenever the students are being taught. He has missed no oppor-tunity for instruction except due to his own inattention."

"Are you suggesting my son is stupid?" Mrs. Mullen's face turned red. Pray she did not suffer an apoplexy in her cousin's par-lor!

"Not at all. I am saying he is not an attentive student. Those are hardly the same thing." Inattentive was far less forgivable than stupid, but that probably was not appropriate to bring up just now.

"How would you know? You are not the schoolmaster. What have you to do with any of this?"

"The other boys have all complained he provokes them during their lessons, prevents them from doing their work, and bul-lies them whenever he has the chance." Mary kept her voice clear and level which only seemed to further inflame Mrs. Mullen. Ra-ther the same effect it had on her son.

"How dare you criticize him! You have no place, no right."

"It is I who set him to chopping wood in order to improve his attitude and actions toward the other boys. Hard work is said to instill character—"

"Who are you to disapprove of his character? I should know my own son's character. We have raised him to be a proper gentleman." Mrs. Mullen tossed her head, setting the feathers on her hat quivering.

"The alternative is the liberal application of the cane which I would think would be even more undesirable to you than a bit of honest work."

Mrs. Mullen stomped several steps closer, a few feet from Mary. "You take too much upon yourself, young woman. I am shocked at you, Mrs. Johnstone, allowing her so much liberty in a task you should be administering yourself."

Mrs. Johnstone's eyes narrowed and she stood. Not an omen of good tidings. "I asked her to come specifically to assist me. I have full confidence—"

"Do you mean to say you are not capable of maintaining the boys in your home? I was assured this would be a good situation for him, one in which he would be well-cared for."

Mrs. Lawson jumped to her feet and rushed to Mrs. Mullen. "Calm yourself, cousin. I have every faith in the Johnstones—"

"Well clearly, you have been utterly mistaken and have led me astray. We shall have our son out of that horrible academy this very afternoon, mark my words. And know this. I shall let it be known far and wide the nature of this school. Mr. Johnstone will never, never have any more students. I will see to that." She tossed her head and stormed from the room.

Chapter 7

MRS. LAWSON SHUT the parlor door, wringing her hands and tut-tutting under her breath. "Pray do not take my cousin's state-ments too much to heart. She is high-strung, especially regarding her child. You must appreciate her unique situation."

"And exactly what special circumstance is that?" Mrs. Johnstone's voice honed to a fine edge.

"The boy, Charles I think is his name. He is her only son, her only child. She has had six others, but none survived more than two years, I think. She herself became seriously ill after birthing him, and they both almost died. She is incredibly protective of him as I am sure you can understand. It is what any mother would do under the circumstances, I think." Mrs. Lawson wandered back to her couch.

"She is not the only woman to have lost a child or even several of them. Many of us have been through that and not turned our sons into—well, in any case, she does the boy no good with such coddling. How will he ever survive in the society of men that way?" Mrs. Johnstone lowered herself back into her seat and drummed her fingers along the arm of her chair.

"You must appreciate her feelings, then. You have three sons, do you not?" Had Mrs. Lawson listened at all?

"I do indeed. I also buried as many as she has. Neither of those facts has any bearing on the realities of a man's world. I am well aware of what is demanded from young men in public school—all my boys did their time there. It is far more rigorous than our little academy. She is doing her son no favors."

"You are too harsh. He is her only child." Mrs. Lawson sat down, looking very sad. Was that great sensibility on her part or actual ignorance? It was difficult to distinguish. "It will all sort it-self out. I am sure you can see that and take a little pity on the child. It would be a shame and most unpleasant for everyone if he should be taken from your care."

"Pray forgive me, but I am not sure you have heard what I am saying." Mrs. Johnstone clutched the arm of her chair. The air between them crackled with some sort of uneasy energy.

Mary jumped to her feet. "Excuse me. I have suddenly been struck with a dreadful headache. I must return to the vicarage. You need not leave on my account though, Mrs. Johnstone. I do not wish to ruin your call." She fled the room and the house.

Yes, it was rude. It was probably uncalled for. In all likeli-hood she was making a terrible impression on Mrs. Lawson and would face quite the well-earned tongue lashing from Mrs. John-stone later. But none of that mattered now.

She ran down the path they had followed to Leighton Man-or, veering off at the fork, into the woods. On the main trail, some-one might see her, ask her questions, and that she could not bear. No, a little quiet and privacy in the shelter of the trees was what definitely what she needed.

Certainly there would be none of that when she arrived at the house. The maid and the cook would all have questions; even the man servant often looked to her. Could not the household man-age itself without her for even a little while? And the children, all those little boys. They would be asking her, demanding of her, where she had been and what she had done. They would want to tell her of their morning, probably including the visit from the Mullens, and their impressions of that as well.

She jammed her fists to her temples. No, just no! She could not take it. Not before she had an opportunity to put her thoughts in order. Not before she had an opportunity to refine her mask and fix it in place. She had let it drop at bit since she had been here, away from the intrusions of Longbourn, but now, it would be nec-essary here as well. She wrapped her arms around her waist, rock-ing slightly and breathing hard.

That was a shame, but not surprising. It had been pleasing to let her guard slip and laugh and even joke without wondering when the criticism would begin. How tempting it had been to think this place might be different. It had seemed so. She had wished it so.

But it was not.

The Johnstones had placed their faith in her to assist with the school, and she had made a cake of things. It was worse than that. It could be the downfall of the school itself. To lose all his students would be a difficult blow, one from which he might never recover. It was true, he had a good living, but to provide for the wife and children he might someday have and for his mother, maybe even his sister, it would help to have more. And she had just taken that away from him. She forced her feet to move into the cover of the trees.

Why did she ever think she had it in her to manage young boys? Papa had been completely wrong when he implied because she had taken care of the Gardiner children, she might be able to handle these as well. Why had he done that to her? Why had he set her up to fail?

She stumbled across a log in her path. When had that gotten there? Surely she should have seen it? Even the paths seemed set against her now. What an utterly foolish thought. Grounds did not turn hostile. But maybe they should. Such a mess she had made of things. She paused and sat down on the log, face in her hands.

The Mullen boy had been unruly, out of control, and disre-spectful. None of those traits served anyone well. At least not if they were the middling sort of gentry.

But, in truth, she had no idea of what sort of family Charles Mullen had come from. She had not considered the matter, and it might have been a great mistake. She had assumed since he was being sent to a country parson's school, he was of the same class she came from. But if there were family connections through the Lawsons, then it was possible his family was far wealthier than that.

Sons of very wealthy families were known to live quite wild lifestyles. His behavior might be entirely expected and toler-ated in his class. It seemed odd to think so, but not impossible. It was not as though she had anyone in her circle of acquaintance whom she could ask if it were true.

But if it was, it would explain Mrs. Mullen's horror at her son's treatment. And if she carried through on her threats ….

All Mary's well-meaning efforts would have ruined a man … a man she cared for more than she should … one that she maybe … no, that was not possible … but yes, it was … one whom she loved. She covered her face with her hands and wept, choking and gut-wrenching sobs she could not have controlled had she wanted to.

When she looked up, eyes blurry and sore, the woods had grown dark. The bits of sky she could make out through the trees were gloomy and ominous. Cold wind slapped at her, warning her of what came with it. Of course, a storm was looming. How fitting when her life felt like a chapter of a Gothic novel.

Lightning seared the sky. Ear-shattering thunder rattled the trees hardly a breath later. She needed to find cover immediately. But where was she?

The path she had been following—she had been following a path, had she not? But where was it now? Paths did not just dis-appear—at least when one was not a heroine in a novel, they did not.

There it was, precisely where it was supposed to be! How could she have missed it? Foolish, foolish girl! Now was not the time to allow ridiculous imaginings to take control of her good sense. Another sharp gust cut through the trees. She wrapped her arms around her waist and hurried down the path until it came to a fork.

If only she had noticed the fork when she was rushing headlong into the woods like a sapscull. She closed her eyes. Which side of the fork had she followed here? Surely, she had come down along the right-hand side. That one would lead her out, maybe even before the rain began.

Or perhaps not. Fat drops splashed on leaves and made their way through the canopy. Only a moment later, a deluge poured from the sky. All hope that any of her person would remain dry disappeared. Wind whipped the rain into painful stinging blasts that burned her cheeks and arms.

She should have cleared the woods by now. The fields should be in view. There was a shack not far from the trail where she ought to be able to take refuge. If only she could get past all these trees.

But the forest remained unmoved. If anything, the trees be-came denser and the path less clear. Was it possible she had taken the wrong fork?

She turned to follow the trail back. Lightning flashed, and something flared in the treetops above her as thunder resonated in her bones. A tree snapped and fell, blocking the path ahead. Even if it were the correct path, she dare not take it until the weather passed.

She glanced about, but it was darker than before. Even if there were shelter nearby, she could not make it out. If she left the path now, would she be able to find it later? Probably not. She huddled near a large tree and tried to forget the aching, wet cold that seeped deep into her bones.

By the time the clouds cleared, they revealed a sliver of moon high in the sky. The light was comforting, but not enough to see by. She would have to wait until morning to find her way back. She closed her eyes and flirted with sleep.

Cool morning breezes across her still-damp clothes roused her from a light sleep. Cold, wet, and thirsty. Most everything ached. That is what one got for getting lost in the woods. And, oh yes, she was still lost. At least there was light now, and she might, if she were lucky, be able to find the way back out of this unfortu-nate place.

She stood and looked around, her sodden skirt clinging to her legs like plaster. Was that the faint trace of the path she had followed yesterday? Possibly, hopefully. Nothing else resembled a trail, so she might as well follow it. She rubbed her hands briskly along her soggy sleeves and set off. With so many limbs blown down by the storm, it was difficult to tell where the trail had been. The waterlogged ground proved slippery with mud and dead leaves under her feet, slowing her progress to a crawl.

What if she could not find her way back? Now she was be-ing silly. Surely she would encounter someone who could direct her to Leighton Manor. She could not be that deep into the woods, could she? But what if she encountered—stop! Hysterical thoughts would not help.

Wait, what was that? She held her breath and closed her eyes as though that might improve her hearing.

"Miss! Miss! Miss Bennet!" A high, boyish voice was not too far off.

"Nate, is that you?" she cried, searching through the tree trunks.

A small form broke through the branches. "I found her! She is here!" Nate ran for her and wrapped his arms around her knees. "I am so glad we found you. I was sure we would. We had to, we just had to." He released her and shouted through cupped hands. "I've found her! She is found!"

More boys burst through the trees, followed by Mr. John-stone. Dark circles lined his eyes matched by furrowed and heavy brows. He approached with solid, powerful steps.

"Are you injured?" He looked over her shoulder, avoiding any eye contact.

"No, sir."

"But she is cold and wet!" Nate cried. "Her lips are nearly blue!"

Mr. Johnstone pulled off his coat and wrapped her in it. Oh gracious, how very warm and heavy and comforting it was. Her knees buckled. He caught her as she crumpled to the ground, sweeping her into his arms.

The boys gathered around him, and they began to walk.

"David, Thomas, run ahead and see that Mrs. Johnstone has warm blankets and hot water ready for us."

The two boys sprinted off.

"You do not have to carry me, I can—"

"Do not argue. If I do not carry you, the children will try to do it themselves." He grumbled, still not looking at her.

She rested her head on his shoulder, strong and secure like the rest of him. But, no doubt he was cross, even angry with her. There was no warmth in his voice or eyes. After all she had done, why would he welcome her presence at all?

She swallowed hard and squeezed her eyes shut, trying to ignore the hot rivulets pouring down her cheeks.

Mrs. Johnstone was waiting in the kitchen with a dry, warm blanket and a large cup of hot broth. Mr. Johnstone set her down in front of the fire and saw her wrapped in the blanket before he stalked away. How delicious was the warmth seeping into her mostly numb and heavy limbs, melting away tension, along with most of her thoughts. As soon as she had drunk the broth, Mrs. Johnstone urged her upstairs, helped her into a warm dry night-gown, and tucked her into a warmed bed. Mary fell asleep before Mrs. Johnstone left her room.

When she rose the next day, it was nearly noon given the shadows on the floor. Peeking over the pile of blankets, the cozy little room took shape around her, sunlight sneaking around the drawn curtains. If only she could stay here, nestled warm and snug— forever. But that was hardly realistic. Nothing would change the reality that she had to face the aftermath of yesterday's storm.

She pushed off the covers and sat up. Gracious, it took more effort than it should to do that. She tested each joint in turn. Stiff and achy, one and all. Easing herself off the bed, she tested her strength. Standing was not too bad despite the lingering weari-ness. Slowly, far more slowly than she would have preferred, she tugged open the drapes, allowing the sunbeams to bathe and warm her. She sniffled and searched for a handkerchief in the press next to the window. If all she had to complain for from a night spent in the woods was a stuffy nose, then she was very lucky indeed.

She dressed, albeit sluggishly, listening to the sounds of the children in the schoolroom below stairs. She swallowed hard. Those noises distracted her when she first came, but now the low roar they created was welcome, even comforting. She would miss it when she left. No doubt, that would be soon enough. Surely, it would not be wrong to linger a few more moments and enjoy it.

A quarter of an hour later, she made her way downstairs. Mrs. Johnstone saw her from the parlor and hurried to meet her.

"How are you feeling? You gave us all such a fright." She laced her arm in Mary's.

"A sniffle, but nothing more of concern. Pray forgive me for causing you worry. I had no idea of getting lost in the woods like that. I followed the trail in, but then took the wrong fork back and … and …" She sniffled. No, it would not do to weep.

Mrs. Johnstone patted her hand. "It could have happened to any of us. You seemed so distraught when you dashed out. In that state of mind, distressing things always seem to happen."

"Still, I should not have been so rash. I like to think that is out of character for me. But perhaps I am mistaken." She balled her fist and pressed it against her belly.

"Nonsense, you are as steady a girl as I have ever known. Come, now, let us find you something to break your fast. You must be famished. I know those boys must not have eaten everything in the house, at least not yet." She chuckled under her breath as she trundled toward the kitchen while waving Mary to the dining room.

Mary sat in the chair that had effectively become hers. Near the window, it afforded a commanding view of the boys when they were seated to eat around the scuffed oak table. Funny little chaps, many still struggling with their table manners. Mealtimes seemed to be as much a lesson time as did the school day. Though there were times she missed the more pol-ished conversation around the dining table at Longbourn, there was an element of whimsy—and chaos—that the boys brought to each meal. She dragged her sleeve across her eyes.

"Miss Bennet?" Mr. Johnstone stood in the door-way staring at her, a little breathless. "My mother told me I was wanted imme-diately in the dining room and has taken over supervising the boys as they read. She implied there was a matter most urgent requiring my attention."

"She told me she was off to the kitchen—"

"Excuse me sir," the maid ducked around him, a breakfast tray in her hands. She set it in front of Mary and scuttled away as fast as she could without run-ning.

"It seems as though she succeeded in her errand." His eye-brow rose slightly. "Pray, please, go ahead and eat. Do not let me stop you." He sat down near her. The herbal scent of his shaving oil nearly brought tears to her eyes. She would miss that.

"You must forgive me. I am not sure I have an appetite." She pushed the tray back several inches. "I have no idea what your mother would consider pressing enough to separate you from your students."

He grunted, lips wrinkled into something like a frown. "I am surprised you ran off as you did. I did not expect you to be foolish enough to be lost in the woods."

She shrugged. "Neither did I. I did not exactly leave Leigh-ton with the plan and intention to become lost."

"Very few do, I would suppose. Still, as many times as you have warned the boys to take care not to lose their way, I expected you to be a better example." He drummed his fingers on the table.

"I did, too." She sipped her cup of tea, more for something to do than anything else.

Silence—broken only by the regular sound of his breathing and her occasional sniffle.

But it could not continue all morning. Someone had to break the stillness. It may as well be her. "I pray you and your mother will be able to forgive me. I … I thought I could do much better for all of you. But it seems I am mistaken. I should go back to Longbourn now, before … before there are any more mishaps. I am sure it will be best for you and the children that way. I can write to my father to send the coach as soon as possible, or if you prefer, I … I do not mind purchasing a ticket for the stage bound for Meryton."

"You would ride the public stage by yourself?" His jaw dropped.

"If that is your preference. I can see I am a disruption to the household and I … I understand why you might want to keep that to a minimum after what has happened." She turned away. Though he seemed to be making no effort to meet her gaze, there was no point in taking a chance he might.

"Are you in such a hurry to be rid of us? That you would jeopardize your reputation?" He slapped the table hard enough to rattle her teacup.

"I never suggested I was." She sat up a little straighter.

"It certainly sounded that way to me." Was he growling at her?

"I am only trying to do what is best for your family and your school."

"And how would you know what was best?" He knocked harder on the tabletop.

"I supposed that is an excellent question. I clearly cannot discern such things and should have declined this invitation in the first place. I have been out of place all along." She stood and turned her back to him. "You may thank the attentions of my most affectionate mother for that."

"It seems then you would do well to be rid of us all."

"You have done nothing to suggest otherwise."

"Have I not?" His chair scraped along the wooden floor.

She whirled and met his gaze full on. The eye contact forced her back half a step, but she grasped the back of her chair and stood her ground. If he thought he could intimidate her now, he had forgotten that day in the library, and she would remind him.

A gambit of expressions crossed his face in just a few sec-onds. Finally he looked away, shoulders slumping and mumbling. "I suppose I have not."

"Excuse me?"

"You are right. I have done little to express my opinion of your contributions one way or another. I have been remiss." His head drooped, and he stared at the floor.

She pulled back her shoulders and straightened her spine. "I beg you, spare me your analysis. It is entirely enough to know the damage I have caused with the Mullens. Whatever else I may have done pales by comparison."

"What damage?" His head snapped up, and he gaped at her.

Surely he was not going to force her to recount it all for him. "Mrs. Mullen declares she will remove her son from your charge and ensure no other families ever sent their sons to you again."

"She said what?" His brows knit, but he laughed, deep and long.

"I cannot understand why you should find that so amus-ing." Her hands trembled.

"Because it is completely laughable, that is why. I cannot imagine why you do not find her diverting as well." He touched her hand and bade her to sit once again.

"Perhaps because I was there to listen to her threats. Ap-parently I seem to take the welfare of your establishment far more seriously than you do if you find threats to it so droll. Clearly I have misplaced my loyalties."

He fell heavily into his chair. "You are being tem-peramental and flighty and utterly unlike yourself, and I will not have it. You are a steady and sensible wom-an, and I demand her to return right now."

"You are awfully sure of yourself."

"I can be when I am right."

Oh, that smug, self-satisfied look he wore. Was he inten-tionally being maddening?

"Mrs. Mullen is a hysterical goose. All who know her agree. She is on the verge of ruining that boy for all good society. He has been sent here in the effort to prepare him for the world of men." Mrs. Johnstone had intimated something like that at the manor.

"That is not what she says." Her voice lost a little of its as-surance.

"Of course not, that is what makes her a goose. It is what his father says that matters in this case, con-sidering it is he who is truly in charge of the boy. Once Mrs. Mullen left our parlor, he took the boy out and gave him a sound thrashing for all the trouble he has caused, then took me to task for not birching him bloody myself."

Her jaw dropped, an unattractive expression she could just see in the mirror hanging on the left hand wall. It was not pleasing to look like a trout out of water, but that seemed all she was capa-ble of at the moment.

"I explained I had not done so since sending him to chop wood was far more humbling and more likely to serve the neces-sary purpose." He leaned back and cocked an eyebrow at her.

"You told him that?"

"Indeed. I am pleased with the approach. That is not to say I may not be forced to follow his father's preferences yet, but I am content to watch and see how his attitude changes now that he knows his com-plaints have fallen on unsympathetic ears."

"They are not taking their child from your school or sug-gesting other parents do the same?"

"Hardly. He has even offered me an extra ten pounds to keep Charles during the holidays." He chuckled.

"What did you tell him?" Mary clasped her hands in her lap.

"I have not made an answer yet." He studied the scratches on the table and muttered, "Do you still wish to return to Long-bourn?"

"Do you want me to?"

He threw his head back and rolled his eyes. "Must you ask that question? Is it not obvious?"

Her throat clamped down against any possible word she could speak, and she looked away. Why of all things would he have had to ask that? She slumped into her chair.

He scoured his face with his hands. "I see I have made a muddle of it again."

It would have been nice to be able to reply, but truly what was she to say?

"When things are so apparent to me, I take it for granted everyone can see them. My most affectionate mother has often scolded me that it is a mistake. Perhaps she is right." He dropped to a knee beside her. "Mary Bennet."

Her eyes locked on his—what had he said? How had he addressed her?

"Ah, now you have heard me. Good, I had feared it might be difficult to get through to you." Finally, that smile she had ached to see. He took her hands between his. "You asked me if I wanted you to leave now. I do not want you to leave, ever. This house has never seemed a home until you stepped through that door. You have invaded every part of my life, my home, my liveli-hood, my parish, my family—pleasing even my very particular mother. You have touched every part and made each one better in a way I cannot express. I have admired your spirit and your fire from the moment you fought me for that library book. I have not been able to stop thinking about you since. When you did not come home yesterday," his voice broke, and he gulped. "When you did not come home, I did not know how I would bear it, wandering within these walls without your company. Pray, do not put me through that again, Mary, my Mary. Be my wife."

"What about your sister? Was she not—"

He laughed again. "She will think you a saint for relieving her from the responsibility. She had little desire to come to the country, much less to assist me."

The corner of her lips turned up.

"You will marry me?"

"Yes, I will."

He cupped her face in his hands and kissed her. "I know it is sentimental and perhaps not even sensible to say, but I have nev-er meant anything more. I love you, Mary, and I hope you never forget that."

.

Chapter 8

MRS. JOHNSTONE RECEIVED their news with pleasure and com-plaints that her son had taken far too long in getting on with the matter. He was lucky, in her estimation, that Miss Bennet was a patient young woman who would tolerate all his dithering. Though her words bordered on harsh, her tone was so good-natured Mary could not be offended on her betrothed's behalf. Who would ever have thought she would find favor with her future mother-in-law? Hopefully their reception at Longbourn would be as auspicious.

The next morning proved clear and bright and all things a wonderful morning ought to be. Mrs. Johnstone was only too hap-py to see them off early. The sooner they obtained her father's ap-proval, the sooner they could get themselves wed, and life at Ash-lea Cottage would return to their comfortable routine.

He handed Mary up to the seat of his modest gig. She had never ridden in such a vehicle before. There was something freeing about having the wind in one's face. True, the weather could make it inconvenient and uncomfortable, but more often than not, travel was that in any case. For now she would enjoy the novelty of it all.

The horse clopped steadily along the road. Each step kicked up small rocks and dust and took them closer to Longbourn. She wrung her hands in her lap.

"You are fretting again." He glanced toward her, a mix of concern and amusement in his eyes.

"I suppose I am." She pulled her hands apart and tucked them under her legs.

"You do not honestly expect your father to object, do you? Not after he practically threw us together." He chuckled under his breath. "I will enjoy the distinction of having the only match-making father-in-law I have ever known of."

"I rather credited that act to my mother's attentions, but I suppose as to effect, there is little difference."

He snickered and urged the horse on. "Never fear, I have not failed to give either of our mothers their fair share of the credit for this happy occasion."

"At least your mother had a plausible reason for inviting me to Ashlea Cottage. I am concerned—"

"You need not be. For this purpose, she will find a way to manage the boys whilst we are gone. She does not like the task, but to get you as a daughter, she will persevere. For which I might add, I am quite grateful." He reached over and squeezed her hands. "She has surprised herself by how fond she is of you."

"Exactly what am I to make of that statement?" she har-rumphed playfully.

"That I am indeed a fortunate man, and nothing you say is going to change my mind."

"Are you sure she will be able to—"

"Cope a few weeks until you return? The glow of her suc-cess will help her rise to the occasion. Though I have no doubt she will be only too glad for you to take over after we are married. I have a feeling she might even be planning a brief visit to my brother in town for some relief." He glanced at her. "You have that peculiar look on your face again. What are you thinking?"

"You will not approve." She turned her face aside.

"I understand being weary of your family's med-dling and condescending attitudes. My mother felt sure no woman would pay me notice if she did not force their hand."

"So that is why you chose to start a school? Be-cause your mother was certain it would result in a wife for you? She has unu-sual methods, sir, very un-usual." She pressed her head to his shoulder. "You know, my mother might fall into a fit of vapors if she sees us driving up like this. We are being rather bold, you know."

"I have no qualms if you do not." He winked at her.

"Ah, sir, I know your games. If I say I do not, you will tease me that my mother will delight in our public declaration be-cause it means you will not back out. And if I say I do, you will threaten to turn back be-fore we are seen. Then you will write to my father, and my parents will both come to Hetherington, my mother bringing all the commotion of a circus with her. And if I defer to your better judgement, you will never cease to remind me of all I have said."

He laughed long and deep, the sound she so dearly loved. "I have been warned of the dangers of marrying a clever woman. You are proving every one of those warnings correct. But I am un-daunted, for I have a clever mother and know firsthand what I have asked for." He pressed her shoulder with his. "You still have not told me why you are so anxious."

As usual, he would not permit her evasions. Odd, how cared for it made her feel. "It is silly I suppose, but I dread my mother's reaction. No matter what it is, I know it will be dreadful and embarrassing. She will take credit for 'she will have known just how it would be.' She will compare you to my sisters' husbands which will be awful no matter how she does it. Or she will be effusive in her relief that her least marriageable daughter is fi-nally off her hands."

"You seem to know your mother well."

"You think I exaggerate?"

"I know too well that you do not." His voice turned low and serious. "I wonder how you will feel about living with my mother when you come to know her better."

"I think your mother is ready to relinquish the duties of the household and enjoy the security of knowing all her sons are re-spectably married. That shall ease our way considerably."

"That was not an answer." He harrumphed. The horse snorted in reply. "I assure you it will be well with your parents. See, there is Longbourn. I will show you." He urged the horse into a slow trot.

"Mr. Bennet! Mr. Bennet! You are wanted imme-diately." Mama shrieked as she flurried down the hall like a nervous hen. Was she afraid he might change his mind if Papa did not appear immediately?

Mary glanced up at Mr. Johnstone.

He leaned down, smirking, and whispered, "I said it would be well, not quiet or easy."

Papa trundled out from his bookroom, removing his glasses and blinking. "You have not even taken them to the parlor, Mrs. Bennet? Where is your hos-pitality? Come, Mr. Johnstone, join me in my bookroom whilst my wife expends her power of con-versa-tion—"

He meant interrogation—

"—upon her daughter."

He glanced at Mary, a little apologetic and fol-lowed Papa into the study. No doubt he would have the easier time of things. Truly what more did Papa need to know? Mr. Johnstone had a good living, a suitable home, a good character, and he wanted to marry her. What more did Papa really care about? How like him would it be to draw out the conversa-tion as long as possible to avoid dealing with Mama.

Mama shooed her into the parlor and shut the door behind them.

"So you have an understanding?" Mama stood near the door, hands clasped in anticipation.

"Would I have ridden alone with him all the way here in an open gig otherwise?" She rolled her eyes. No, it was not polite, but no one could be expected to do otherwise under the circumstances.

"Do not be smart with me, miss. You would not be on the verge of marriage without my attentions.

You should be thanking me, not putting on airs." Mama bustled to her favorite chair near the tea table.

Mary smiled and nodded as she made her way to her pre-ferred seat. At least she might be comfortable while biting her tongue and biding her time.

Mama settled into her chair, a knowing look in her eye. "So you think you got him yourself? I was the one who invited him to dinner. I was the one who suggested you two study together. How else would you have spent so much time together if it were not for my interventions—"

"Perhaps Mrs. Johnstone's invitation to stay with them might have had some effect." Mary squeezed her eyes shut. She should not have said such a thing, should not have tried to provoke Mama so. It was not kind and probably not smart, either.

Mama stopped midsentence and stared at her, jaw agape. "You truly believe an effort on her part to put you two together?"

"What else would you call it?" Was she really arguing which mother had done more match-making?

"The woman is half-deaf and blind and her mind half-gone. I was surprised she had enough wits about her to write you a letter of invitation at all."

Which would also require the power of sight to accomplish. Best not mention that to Mama just now.

"I will concede that it is fortunate she saw you as able to help with something clearly disagreeable." Mama punctuated each syllable with her hands. "That will make it much easier for you to live with her. But the important thing is you made proper use of the time together—"

"Do you to wish to hear of his home, or the school he has there?"

"There is plenty of time to talk about those matters later. Mrs. Daring has already assured me that the Hetherington Vicarage is quite suitable. That is enough for me right now. More important, we must consider your wedding clothes. You will have no need of the finery Jane and Lizzy required, but still a trip to London is in order. With your Uncle Gardiner's help, I cannot imagine it will take—"

"Mama, Mr. Johnstone will speak to Mr. Daring about reading our banns starting this week. We will wed as soon as they have been read three times."

"Why the rush child?" Mama gasped and turned pale. "You do not fear you are—"

"Mama! What are you suggesting? No, absolutely not. He has a school to run, and his mother is not up to the task of helping him. He needs me there as soon as possible to help with the stu-dents."

"Oh, well, I suppose it cannot be helped then. I insist you be married from Longbourn though. I have given the wedding breakfast a great deal of thought whilst you have been away ...."

Mary smiled and nodded as Mama waxed long about the menu for the wedding breakfast and the guest list. Though it might not be exactly what she would want, there was little point in argu-ing. As long as they could leave early enough to get to Hetherington that evening, whatever Mama insisted upon would be tolerable.

Hill handed Mary a box containing a medium-sized bride's cake. The dear woman had seen to it that an entire extra cake was baked for them to bring back to the vicarage to share with the chil-dren and Mrs.

Johnstone. Mama did not understand the need, but Hill did, and Mary would be ever grateful.

Though Mama's guests still enjoyed Longbourn's hospitali-ty, it was time for the guests of honor to de-part. Mary and Percy—it was good to be able to call him that now—took their leave and headed for his waiting gig. Her parents followed them out the front door, Mama dabbing her eyes with her handkerchief.

Mary blinked in the bright sun. It was still high enough in the sky that they would arrive in Hether-ington with plenty of day-light to spare. Fluffy clouds dotted the sky—the happy friendly sort, not the kind that threatened rain and would keep them from their destination. All in all, it seemed an ideal morning for travel-ing, especially when it was to one's new home with the man she loved.

"Oh, my dear girl! Whatever will I do? How will I manage the dearth of female company here? With all four of you gone—"

Mary cringed. Her company had never seemed important before. "I am sure you will find Kitty's companionship quite suffi-cient."

"How can you say such a thing? You are going in-to a neighborhood where you know no one, where you have no friends. I dread sending you into so iso-lated a state."

How odd it never seemed to matter that was exact-ly what happened with Jane, Lizzy, and Lydia. "I met a great number of people whilst I stayed in at the vic-arage. I have no concerns at all."

"That is because you do not know how lonely a woman can become. I insist, for your sake, bring Kit-ty with you. I know she can be a great help to you. Living with a man you hardly know is—"

"I know him far better than you think—and you have taken credit for that, as I recall. Why do you not relax in the fruits of your labors now and enjoy Kitty's camaraderie for yourself?"

Mama dismissed her remark with a sharp wave. "Really, it is nothing. I can have her packed and there tomorrow afternoon with no trouble."

"Truly, it is better for her here."

"I insist. I cannot be selfish with my girls."

"Hetherington is a small village, much smaller than Mery-ton. There are few young men there, especially with the sort of prospects you would hope for in a son. There is nothing there for her. She would be much better off with Jane or Elizabeth who could see her introduced to a much wider acquaintance than I will ever have."

Mama sniffed and snorted and rolled her eyes. "Well, if you put it that way."

"Come, Mrs. Johnstone, we must away." He beckoned to her from the gig.

Mary curtsied to Mama and rushed to him. He handed her up into the gig, and they were off.

"Well that proved more difficult than I expected," he mut-tered.

"Indeed? What did Papa have to say?"

"He suggested your mother might be interested in visiting the vicarage soon. After all, she hardly got to meet my mother whilst she was staying with Mrs. Daring."

"I do not imagine you supported the notion."

"Hardly."

"Mama was insisting I bring Kitty with us, to … ah … as-sist me in my transition and keep me from being lonely."

He stared at her wide-eyed as though afraid to ask.

"Calm your fears. I made it very clear there were no young men in Hetherington for Kitty." She smoothed her skirt over her lap.

"Do you want your sister to stay with us?"

"Excuse me?"

"If you refused on my behalf … I just do not want to deny you anything that might make things easier for you." He sneaked a quick glance at her.

The attitude was dear, to be sure, but … "What leads you to believe my sister would make things easier for me?"

"It is a done thing among many I have known."

"Perhaps by some. But not by me. You are already bringing me into a houseful of children. I hardly need another one."

"Your sister is no child."

"You do not know Kitty very well, do you?" She har-rumphed. "She is silly and flighty and frivolous. She would be bored to death with the shops in Hetherington which she certainly would visit every day. That is one of her favorite activities, after all. As for finding any assistance in her, you can drive that thought from your mind. She is—utterly useless is perhaps too strong so I shall not say that—let us say she is not likely to be helpful. She does not like to manage a household and is scarcely sympathetic to children. If she must work, she complains bitterly and leaves tasks half-done—hardly the example I want to set for our young charges. She of all of us needs a wealthy husband to deliver her from all those tasks she hates."

"Do you mind having a houseful of other people's children? You know, you did far more with them than anyone could have expected. If you do not wish to engage with them at that level once we return, there is nothing says you have to. They do not need to be constantly watched over. They arc old enough to leave home. If their parents were poorer, many of them would be appren-ticed or working by now. You do not need—"

She laid her hand on his. "Pray stop, just stop. I know they are too old to be mothered, and yet, I am fond of them. I interact with them because I like them, and I like to do it. It pleases me to believe Charles' behavior has become more tolerable since I inter-vened."

"Indeed, it has. But there is something to be said for the youngsters learning how to manage bullies on their own, for they will have to in the future."

"Do you want me to stop then? To ignore the children as paying tenants and nothing more?"

"Hardly," he mumbled under his breath. "You have been a great help to me."

"Then stop trying to be so agreeable and allow me to do that."

"Yes, Mrs. Johnstone." He flashed his eyebrows and winked at her.

"Cheeky man." She rolled her eyes and leaned against his shoulder.

"Obstinate, headstrong girl."

"I take that as a compliment, sir."

"One of many that I hope you will soon accustom yourself to."

Author's Note

Early Education of up and coming Gentlemen

In all well-regulated states, the two principal points in view in the education of youth, ought to be, first, to make them good men, good members of the universal society of mankind; and in the next place to frame their minds in such a manner, as to make them most useful to that society to which they more immediately belong; and to shape their talents, in such a way, as will render them most serviceable to the support of that government, under which they were born, and on the strength and vigour of which, the well-being of every individual, in some measure depends. (Sheridan, 1756)

Although popular sentiments favored the education of youth (read here, male youth; female education would not be considered worthwhile yet for quite some time), no one really argued for state provided education for middle and upper class children before 1850. (Brown, 2011) So the task was left entirely in the hands of the parents. Although considerable effort and activity went into educating up and coming gentlemen (gentleboys?), it was hardly standardized, depending entirely on the preferences and means of his family.

Early education

On the whole, early education in the home was preferred. Mothers and governesses would provide a boy's first education, often teaching him the basics of reading and writing. Usually by the age of seven he would graduate from being taught by women to being educated by men. There were no standards of how this worked though. The specific details varied by family and by social class.

A male tutor might be brought into the home to teach the child, preparing him for the next step in his education. This could continue for just a few years until the boy was deemed ready for a boarding school, or it could continue until he was ready for university study. Alternatively, a boy might be sent to a local scholar, often a clergyman, for lessons as a day student. Many clergymen also took such students on as boarders, running small schools to supplement their income teaching anywhere for half a dozen to two dozen students. The choice of option depended on the educational philosophy of the family, usually the father. (Selwyn 2010) This definitely makes me wonder how Darcy's father would have seen to his education.

Preparatory Schools

These smaller schools, which routinely took boys in the 7 to 13 year old age range, were often referred to as preparatory schools, preparing boys for the larger public schools that often preceded entry into the universities.

These schools were usually held in the schoolmaster's home. Jane Austen's father, Rev. George Austen conducted such a school out of the vicarage in Steventon beginning in 1793. His living as a vicar was £230 a year. He charged £35 per term for each of his student boarders. It is easy to see how taking even just a few students could substantially augment his family's income. The work though did not fall on him alone. His wife cooked, cleaned, sewed, and mother-henned the boys in her care, much like a surrogate mother. (Sanborrn, 2016)

In larger schools where the teaching staff consisted of ordained clergymen, teachers could make as much as £200-400 a year, giving them a comfortably middle class income. (Davidoff 2002) Headmasters in such schools, especially if scholars themselves, might enjoy a position of respect and distinction in local society. (Selwyn 2010)

By modern standards, preparatory school curriculum was very limited. It consisted mainly of Latin and Greek classical texts (both prose and verse), modern and ancient history, some mathematics, and the use of globes to locate nations. French and Italian might be taught as extras (for additional fees), along with handwriting, dancing, drawing and a smattering of scientific subjects. (Le Faye, 2002) No curriculum standards existed, so what might actually be taught varied widely and there was no guarantee that a particular teacher was actually well versed in the subjects he taught.

Teachers in these preparatory schools were most often clergymen or failed ordinals. There were far more men ordained than there were livings to provide for them. In 1805, it was estimated that up to 45% of those ordained never found a church living and were forced to work as (usually highly underpaid) curates for men who had a living, or to try their hand at teaching or take up another occupation entirely outside the church. (Southam, 2005)

After their education in these preparatory schools, boys might then progress to a public school.

Public Schools

Public schools were public in the sense that boys were taught in groups outside of their private homes, not in the sense that these institutions were funded by public funds. Ironically, they were also considered public because any member of the public who could afford to attend (or rather his parents could afford it) could attend.

A number of public schools existed, but the landed elite in particular chose to send their sons to a select number of these schools: Eton, Harrow, Winchester, Westminster, Rugby, Charterhouse and Shrewsbury. (Adkins, 2013) The exact timing and duration of a boy's stay at school varied greatly. Some were sent as young as age seven and stayed until age eighteen. More commonly boys started public schools around age thirteen and stayed about five years.

Though Regency era education was very different

from modern education, two factors in particular seem to distinguish it most from modern schooling: the curriculum taught and the life style of the students.

What was Taught

Students were expected to know some Latin upon arrival to public school. "The first two years of their education was entirely a study of Latin–memorizing, reciting, reading, and answering set questions in that language.... Thus they learned to be confident public speakers, first in Latin, then in classical Greek and finally in English." (Bennetts 2010) These studies also developed an understanding of the moral and philosophical issues brought up by the classical thinkers and a literary appreciation of poetry and prose. Dancing, fencing and other sports also featured in some curriculums.

What was notably absent from both public school and university educations were courses on anything the modern mind would consider practical. Since these establishments catered to gentlemen who were not destined to actually work for their living, courses like bookkeeping or land management that might equip them for jobs (oh the horror!) were relegated to schools that catered to the sons of men in trade. (Selwyn 2010)

Life in public school

Students at public schools either boarded at the school itself or in town at boarding houses known as 'Dame's Houses' usually overseen by a 'Dame' or landlady. In the early 1800s, about thirteen such houses were associated with Eton. Although school life was very regimented, with school days running from six in the morning until eight in the evening, there was actually very little direct supervision over the boys. They were often left to fend for themselves. Once they entered public school, most boys spent the majority of their year at school, with only a few weeks of holidays spent back at home during the year.

With a strong economic incentive to admit as many students as possible, public schools were often so crowded that even beds were shared by two or more boys at the same time. The same incentives also influenced the quantity and quality of food made available to the students. Those with pocket money frequently supplemented their rations at local shops. (Brander, 1973)

Under such conditions, it was no surprise that public school culture was wild. Almost no limits were placed to the amount the boys could drink, gamble, fight and indulge any sexual bent with maid servants, local prostitutes, and girls living in town. Even the institution of prefects (older boys in charge of younger ones) did little to curb the out of control behavior. " … Most schools suffered occasional rebellions, or mutinies, resulting in mass expulsions or floggings. In 1797, Dr. Ingles, headmaster of Rugby, had his door blown open by gunpowder. The boys at Harrow were even more ambitious, setting up a road block and blowing up one of the governor's carriage." (Brander, 1973)

Bullying and Brutality

Not only was dissolute, licentious behavior the norm, bullying and brutality were expected. Corporal punishment consisting of flogging with a birch, or caning with a rod until blood was drawn from the bare buttocks, was regarded as the normal and accepted punishment for transgressions. Such punishments were frequently delivered in public, adding additional humiliation to the experience.

Not only was brutality dished out from the masters to the students, older boys were put in charge of younger ones and permitted to order them about and punish them with beatings just as the school masters did. Depending on the sorts of friends a boy did or did not make and how he got on with others, especially older students, a boy's public school years could be very testing indeed.

Why was it tolerated?

If public schools could be so bad, why did not parents intervene? Why would a father who had suffered through such school days send his son into a place that brutalized him?

In short, such an environment was regarded as essential for inculcating the toughness and fortitude men needed to perform their social roles. "Educators and parents subscribed to the principle that one was fit to command only after one had learned to obey. And those young boys of the gentry and nobility were there to learn their place and destiny in England's highly structured society." (Laudermilk, 1989)

So, even if a boy had been able to appeal to parents for help, he would have been unlikely to receive either assistance or sympathy. At a very tender age, he was literally on his own, to survive the experience in whatever way he could. Is it any wonder that the friends a boy made during his time in public school were often strong allies for a lifetime?

References

Adkins, Roy, and Lesley Adkins. *Jane Austen's England.* Viking, 2013.

Austen, Jane, and David M. Shapard. *The Annotated Persuasion.* New York: Anchor Books, 2010.

Bennetts, M.M. "A gentleman's education." M.M. Bennets. July 20, 2010. Accessed October 5, 2016. https://mmbennetts.wordpress.com/2010/07/27/a-gentlemans-education/

Brander, Michael. *The Georgian Gentleman.* Glasgow: University Press, 1973.

Brown, Richard. "Educating the middle-classes 1800-1870. Looking at History." Accessed October 29, 2016. http://richardjohnbr.blogspot.com/2011/02/educating-middle-classes-1800-1870.html>

Davidoff, Leonore, and Catherine Hall. *Family Fortunes: Men and Women of the English Middle Class, 1780-1850.* Chicago: University of Chicago Press, 1987.

Day, Malcom. *Voices from the World of Jane Austen.* David and Charles, 2006.

Evans, Bronwen. "Eton College During the Regency." Era. Collette Cameron. May, 9, 2015. Accessed

October 3, 2016.

https://collettecameron.com/2015/09/eton-college-during-the-regency-era/

Glover, Anne. "Regency Culture and Society: Harrow." Regency Reader. November, 15, 2013. Accessed October 10, 2016.

http://www.regrom.com/2013/11/15/regency-culture-and-society-harrow/

Laudermilk, Sharon H., and Teresa L. Hamlin. *The Regency Companion*. New York: Garland, 1989.

LeFaye, Deirdre. *Jane Austen: The World of Her Novels.* New York: Abrams, 2002.

Locke, John. *Some Thoughts concerning Education*. London, 1693.

Morris, Diane H. "I Am Illiterate by Regency Standards." Moorgate Books. Thursday, October 8, 2015. Accessed May 22, 2017.

http://www.moorgatebooks.com/10/i-am-illiterate-by-regency-standards/

Sanborn, Vic. "19th Century Learning Academies and Boarding Schools: An Eyewitness Account" Jane Austen's World. August 1, 20012. Accessed October 28, 2016.

https://janeaustensworld.wordpress.com/tag/regency-schooling

Selwyn, David. *Jane Austen and Children*. London: Continuum, 2010.

Sheridan, Thomas. *British Education*. London: R. and J. Dodeley, 1756.

Southam, Brian . "Professions," in *Jane Austen in Context.* edited by Janet Todd, p 366-376. Cambridge, UK: Cambridge University Press, 2005.

Sullivan, Margaret C., and Kathryn Rathke. *The Jane Austen Handbook: Proper Life Skills from Regency England.* Philadelphia, PA: Quirk Books, 2007.

Acknowledgments

So many people have helped me along the journey taking this from an idea to a reality.

Debbie, Susanne and Ruth thank you so much for cold reading, proof reading and being honest!

And my dear friend Cathy, my biggest cheerleader, you have kept me from chickening out more than once!

And my sweet sister Gerri who believed in even those first attempts that now live in the file drawer!

Thank you!

Other Books by Maria Grace

Remember the Past
The Darcy Brothers

A Jane Austen Regency Life Series:
A Jane Austen Christmas: Regency Christmas Traditions
Courtship and Marriage in Jane Austen's World
How Jane Austen Kept her Cook: An A to Z History of Georgian Ice Cream

Jane Austen's Dragons Series:
A Proper Introduction to Dragons
Pemberley: Mr. Darcy's Dragon
Longbourn: Dragon Entail
Netherfield:Rogue Dragon

The Queen of Rosings Park Series:
Mistaking Her Character
The Trouble to Check Her
A Less Agreeable Man

Sweet Tea Stories:
A Spot of Sweet Tea: Hopes and Beginnings (short story anthology)
Snowbound at Hartfield
A Most Affectionate Mother

Darcy Family Christmas Series:
Darcy and Elizabeth: Christmas 1811
The Darcy's First Christmas
From Admiration to Love

On Line Exclusives at:

Bonus and deleted scenes
Regency Life Series

Free e-books:
Four Days in April
Half Agony, Half Hope: New Reflections on Persuasion
Rising Waters: Hurricane Harvey Memoirs
Lady Catherine's Cat
The Scenes Jane Austen Never Wrote: First Anniversaries
Bits of Bobbin Lace

About the Author

Though Maria Grace has been writing fiction since she was ten years old, those early efforts happily reside in a file drawer and are unlikely to see the light of day again. After penning five file-drawer novels in high school, she took a break from writing to pursue college and earn her doctorate in Educational Psychology. After 16 years of university teaching, she returned to her first love, fiction writing.

She has one husband and one grandson, two graduate degrees and two black belts, three sons, four undergraduate majors, five nieces, written six different series, built seven websites, started her eighth year blogging on Random Bits of Fascination, sewn nine Regency era costumes, and shared her life with ten cats.

She can be contacted at:

author.MariaGrace@gmail.com

Facebook:
http://facebook.com/AuthorMariaGrace

On Amazon.com:
http://amazon.com/author/mariagrace

Random Bits of Fascination
(http://RandomBitsofFascination.com)

Austen Variations (http://AustenVariations.com)

English Historical Fiction Authors
(http://EnglshHistoryAuthors.blogspot.com)

White Soup Press (http://whitesouppress.com/)

On Twitter @WriteMariaGrace

On Pinterest: http://pinterest.com/mariagrace423/

Printed in Great Britain
by Amazon